Jelena Lengold

FAIRGROUND MAGICIAN

Translated from the Serbian by
Celia Hawkesworth

About the author:

Jelena Lengold is a storyteller, novelist and a poet. She has published six books of poetry, one novel (Baltimore, 2003, 2011) and four books of stories, including *Pokisli lavovi* (Rain-soaked Lions, 1994), *Lift* (Lift, 1999) and *Vašarski mađioničar* (The Fairground Magician, 2008, 2009). She has been represented in several anthologies of poetry and stories, and her works have been translated into several languages. Lengold worked as a journalist and an editor for ten years in the cultural department of Radio Belgrade. She then worked as a project coordinator in the Conflict Management programme of Nansenskolen Humanistic Academy in Lillehammer, Norway. She now lives and writes in Belgrade, Serbia.

About the translator:

Celia Hawkesworth taught Serbian and Croatian at the School of Slavonic and East European Studies, University College, London, 1971-2002. She has published numerous articles and several books on Serbian, Croatian, and Bosnian literature, including the studies *Ivo Andrić: Bridge between East and West* (Athlone Press, 1984); *Voices in the Shadows: Women and Verbal Art in Serbia and Bosnia* (CEU Press, 2000); and *Zagreb: A Cultural History* (Oxford University Press, 2007). Her translations of Dubravka Ugresić's *The Museum of Unconditional Surrender* was short-listed for the Weidenfeld Prize for Literary Translation, and *The Culture of Lies* won the Heldt Prize for Translation in 1999. This is her second book for Istros Books, the first being *Odohohol & Cally Rascal* by Matko Sršen.

First published in 2013 by
Istros Books
London, United Kingdom
www.istrosbooks.com

© Jelena Lengold, 2013
Translation ©Celia Hawkesworth, 2013
Artwork & Design@Milos Miljkovich, 2013
Graphic Designer/Web Developer -
miljkovicmisa@gmail.com

This novel was first published in Serbian as Vašarski
mađioničar, *Archipelag, Belgrade, 2008*
The right of Jelena Lengold to be identified as the
author of this work has been asserted in accordance
with the Copyright, Designs and Patents Act, 1988

ISBN: 978-1908236104
Printed in England by
CMP (UK) , Poole, Dorset
www.cmp-uk.com

Education and Culture DG

Culture Programme

This project has been funded with support from
the European Commission. This publication reflects
the views only of the author, and the Commission
cannot be held responsible for any use which may be
made of the information contained therein.

'Listen, I am going to impart to you once again a comfortless truth, and I shall continue to do so until you become entirely aware: we are helpless, we give in to inertia, people never cease to wound us. The world oppresses us. Like an insupportable itch. And an itch, they say, is a mild pain.'

Mihajlo Pantić, from the story 'What I am to myself'

'... a certain relaxation in realising that we are all destined to be losers, only each of us has a different way of allocating the bitter taste of failure.'

Dragan Velikić, *The Russian Window*

CONTENTS

That could have been me

Had I been born just a few minutes earlier, I could have been Victor. Every time a plane takes off and gravity presses me into my seat, I regret that I am not.

Victor owns a little chemist's shop, on the edge of town. On one side of his shop, there is a watchmaker. On the other, a newsagent where he buys his paper every morning. Even while he was still studying pharmacology, Victor dreamed of arranging various little bottles of medicines on clean white shelves and knowing the exact function and dosage of each individual remedy.

There was something about medicines that had fascinated him since his childhood. He remembered that his grandparents always had lots of medicines in their house. In the kitchen there were two large drawers full of them and, as a child, Victor used to open up that world of danger and prohibition the way some other children open books of fairy-tales.

There were ordinary tablets, then capsules of various colours, different kinds of ointment, red rolls of sticking plaster, a small transparent bottle of iodine with a little cork stopper, nose drops, eye drops, a thermometer in a dilapidated cardboard box, plasters for his grandmother's blisters, liquid smelling of peppermint sweets that was rubbed into the forehead of anyone with a headache. There were remedies which were long past their sell-by date, but his grandparents did not discard them because you never knew when you might need something.

Victor was convinced that it was precisely there, standing in front of that drawer, that he had learned to read, opening each individual box and reading the usage of each medicine.

His favourite game was collecting various different capsules in one little bottle. And there were all kinds of combinations: there were transparent capsules through which granules could be seen, then there were those that hid their contents behind opaque plastic, there were some small and some larger capsules, and the more different specimens he could find, the richer he felt he was. He would take a capsule in his hand, shake it slowly by his ear and listen to the tiny granules rattling. Not all the capsules rattled in the same way. While he was still a child, Victor set himself the task of knowing, simply by its sound, with his eyes shut, which remedy he was holding in his hand.

His grandmother was appalled by his collection and kept reminding him that on no account must he ever swallow any of the medicines, which Victor thought then was an entirely senseless remark, because trying the remedies was not remotely the point; what mattered was possessing them and feeling them under his fingers, telling one from another and, in his childish way, controlling them.

He controlled the medicines, and the medicines controlled life. And death. About which no one ever spoke in those days, but it was present in a very obvious way in those big, extremely heavy drawers.

Later, when Victor realised his childhood dream and opened his chemist's shop, everything seemed to have fallen into place. Quite simply, he would get up in the morning and the only thing he wanted to do was to go to the shop. And he would spend hour after hour there, perfectly contented, and when the time came to close the shop, he would not feel that he was being released from an unpleasant daily burden. On the contrary, his departure for home was an inevitable evil that separated him, only temporarily, from what he really loved.

That's what I'm talking about.

That man – Victor – could easily have been me. As I consider his life, tidily arranged on shelves, I understand, without a shred of horror, that I would cope with that system quite comfortably. I recognise that smell. I recognise that endless repetition of the identical, the benign expectation of the next person who might come into the chemist's shop and hand me a piece of paper with a prescription. I recognise that frantic hope that for everything in the world that hurts you there must be an appropriate remedy.

Sometimes I come home and it seems to me that life is eluding me, that I will never manage it all. It is all deadlines, complex relationships, unfinished business, unclear outlines, travel to organise meetings where you have to be self-possessed. Sometimes it all really does seem too much for just one life. Then I take a diazepam. And have a shower. The minutes slip by, the warm water cascades over me – I can feel it – dissolving that precious chemical in me. Slowly, it all slips away down the plughole. All those scowling faces, all those ambiguous words, all those tense conversations. The sharp edges soften. Nothing is quite as urgent or uncertain any more. Gradually colours return. After some ten minutes life looks fundamentally different. And fundamentally more bearable.

But alas, no. I was not born a few minutes earlier and I did not become Victor. I was born at precisely the moment when those who are forever hurrying somewhere and often use aeroplanes are born.

It might seem irrational to some, that a person who has constantly to fly should be constantly afraid of flying. But that is just a superficial way of looking at it. Because, what would be the point of the journey if not fear?

We do not, in fact, ever know what our lives, made up of all those desires and fears, will degenerate into. For instance, mine has been mainly governed by the elements. The elements and chance. The elements, chance and fate.

And so, for those two or three hours, I devote myself to my fear. Planes are not sufficiently comfortable for sleeping, or reading, or watching films. OK, I could always hook one of those MP3 players into my ears and put my laptop on my knee, but – that's not me. No one else needs to know, I would be able to deceive myself. I am far better at planning my own violent death, than typing a half-yearly financial report at a height of eight thousand metres.

And what is the big deal about these players and headsets? Music used to be something that was *heard*! Something you inevitably shared with everyone around you who had ears. When the radio was on, when someone sang, when there was a record on the gramophone, there was no possibility of it not being heard. That was the essence of music. Neighbours would bang on your walls, they would come to ask you to turn it down, they would summon the police to your door, you would wallpaper your room with egg cartons. That all happened precisely because music was audible.

When you knew what people listened to, you knew what they were like, where they came from, *what stage they were at,* what was bothering them ... But now you don't know a thing. These people with inaudible music in their ears look to me more like people who do not hide the fact that they want to cut themselves off – from me, of course, who else! – anymore than authentic music lovers. I would not be surprised if what they were listening to through those headsets was, in fact, nothing, or just some kind of plop, plop, plop, a recording of a stalactite dripping in a cave in the Himalayas, or some such perversion. That is what people with headsets are like. Very strange.

A friend of mine, a pianist, recently told me the saddest thing: there are now even soundless pianos! The plane is just flying into a black cloud, a metallic voice informs us that we must fasten our seatbelts because we are encountering a little turbulence, and I am imagining well-disciplined strings somewhere in the depths of a piano that play somehow inside themselves. The pianist sits at the piano, making all those usual movements, like Domenico Cimarosa, pulling all those faces, but without the slightest sound. Just headsets and a contented neighbourhood. The pianist plays and plays and plays and nothing happens. Except in his ears. The peace of those around is the priority.

Then there is another crazy thing. I know of several countries already where there are very strange cinemas. I do not know whether they can be called cinemas, because – there is no film. You go in, buy your ticket, sit down; the seats are always very comfortable, the light is discreet and not oppressive, and all that can be heard for the next few hours is just soft, soothing music. You would not believe it, there are countries where cinemas like that are full all day long. There is always someone who wants just to sit for a couple of hours, listening to some tedious Clayderman, or something like that, that you otherwise only hear in a lift.

I have to say that I think these people are even odder than the ones with headsets. These people also shut themselves up in order to listen to music discreetly, politically correctly, but they have added two more elements to the whole thing: relaxation, which is presumably their psychoanalyst's first recommendation, and shutting themselves up in a ghetto of people like themselves.

I dare not even imagine what the next stage might be. How listening to music will look in the future.

But on the other hand, the last thing I want is to sound nostalgic for the past. Like one of those people for whom the way things *used to be* was always better. Like hell it was better! Of course it was not. I would not swap all this technology for a single ethnographic museum in the world. Shameful, perhaps, but true. Still, I am sometimes afraid that some things are too turned inwards, too far from the rest of quiet humanity, even for my taste.

And that is why I do not listen to music in planes; that is what I wanted to say. If we cannot all listen, if at least two or three rows cannot sway to the same rhythm, then it is no real fun.

So I sit and say nothing. They say nothing, I say nothing. They stare at the advertisement on the seat in front of them. So do I.

I know some people who have been trying to

persuade me for years that they simply *adore* flying! They ask for a window seat, make that contented face when they hear the enormous wheels gather speed, they look happy and smiley as though someone was tickling them where they like it. But I do not see what there is to adore. One can be indifferent to flying, it can be accepted as a necessary evil, it can be overcome, but the idea of adoring it I find truly odd.

How could I possibly adore the fact that I am ten thousand metres up in the air, and I am not a bird, or a cloud, or a cosmonaut? Or should I be enjoying the height I am at *just because* I am none of those things?

I don't know, I was never much good at that 'just because' kind of reason. Consider that a serious flaw in my character. I do not like anything that is 'despite'. I am scared of 'despite' situations. I do my best to avoid them. The stuff that is logical is not that easy, if you ask me. 'Despite' is more than I can handle. I leave that to those who are bored and for whom what is implicit is too narrow.

Ping! The little red light over our heads has gone out. We may unfasten our belts. The world below, which ought to be real, can be seen again, those black mountain peaks again. That is what life looks like from up here. Black and aggressively pointed.

That makes me think of mountain-climbers. Those extreme maniacs, who clamber onto high mountain peaks, through the wind and bitter cold. They emerge from their warm room, from their warm hotel, move away from the fireplace, leave their cup of tea and put on that spaceman's outfit, take their poles, fling a hundred kilograms of all kinds of nails onto their backs and set off. Well rubbed with creams to prevent their fingers and ears falling off.

There is no way that anyone will persuade me this is normal behaviour. There is no way that you will explain to me that this is precisely why humanity has progressed, because of people like that. I do not believe it.

Then I do, after all, open my newspaper, while I wait for the refreshments trolley to reach my seat. I turn the pages, turn, turn, and then suddenly that news item. And their photographs. *'They killed their newborn baby.'* I look at their faces. I could pass faces like that and have no idea. A young woman and her father.

A strategically body-built steward appears beside me. What would I like?

I would like to cry, but it would not be right to say that. I say:

'Coffee.'

'With milk or without?' he asks.

And suddenly someone cares how I am going to drink my coffee.

She already had two children, it says, from her first marriage. She lives with her father and children. She does not have a job, her father supports her. She got pregnant out of wedlock with a lad from a neighbouring village. She did not have the money for an abortion. Her father insisted that she leave hospital the day after she gave birth. She held her baby in her arms, a healthy little boy weighing four and a half kilos.

I try to comfort myself. I try to tell myself that a healthy little boy one day old and weighing four and a half kilos does not have that much consciousness.

The father drove her into a forest. He cleared

grass and leaves with his hands. He allowed her to feed her baby one last time. And then he took the little boy and buried him. Alive.

She says that she did not dare oppose her father.

He says that he did not have the money to support a third child.

The court experts say that the baby was probably eaten by wild dogs in the forest.

The neighbours say that they knew she was pregnant and saw that she came back without a baby.

The steward is still waiting.

I say: 'With milk.'

I need something sweet. As sweet as possible. Intolerably sweet. Something capable of burying this feeling.

I have this appalling tendency to torment myself by visualising everything that hurts me. I imagine the baby's little lips on his mother's nipple, for the last time. I imagine the smell of the torn up grass and leaves. I imagine the ghostly sound that can be heard under the grass as the two of them walk away. I catch myself in a strange gesture, I rock backwards and forwards, like Hitler at that famous Olympics, I rock like that, trying not to burst into tears up here over some unknown mountain and hoping that my coffee with milk will be sufficiently warm and sufficiently sweet and that I shall somehow shake this news item from myself.

In the whole story, I feel least hate for the wild forest dogs. I imagine that they reached the baby, that they dug the grass and leaves away, that they smelled the fine aroma of milk and newborn tears and that they took that all into themselves in two tender bites and so put an end to the sacred suffering.

In some forest, perhaps precisely the black one lying ten kilometres beneath me, a sated dog is running about. Here, a little higher up, I sit and drink coffee with milk.

There is no drink that would be sweet enough for something like this. I breathe deeply and look at the sky all around me. Blue, translucent, fresh.

There is no way that I shall be giving up smoking this week.

As soon as this damned plane liberates me, I shall light a cigarette. Victor would not do that, I know, but I am not Victor and I will have to.

There are two young women beside me, talking without drawing breath. I realise that now. One of them is holding her cup just the way I like to, with both hands. As though it is warming her. That always moves me.

I only catch fragments of their conversation:

"... Now I get it. He spent a long time juggling all those three balls in the air, until he realised that he would have to drop one of them, otherwise he'd lose them all. It turned out that it was me who was the ball he decided to drop ..."

"... The two of them cut that huge wedding cake together, clumsily and everyone went wild with enthusiasm, cameras flashing, relatives sighing, sobbing! I mean, what's the big deal? They cut an ordinary cake, i.e. custard, beaten eggs, cream, soft, it's not as if they cut through reinforced concrete for them to go so crazy! I mean, really ..."

"... When you whisk up instant coffee, there is a precise number of drops of water that need to be added! One drop too many and it's no longer right. It's just a shapeless mass. However hard you try and keep whisking, that mixture is never going to turn white under your hand. It just won't obey you any more ..."

"... Don't talk him up! Don't make him better and more interesting than he really is! On the contrary, give him fewer chances than others. Brush out of his repertoire even something he does have. Then, if he manages to get through all of that – then he's really quite a guy ... "

"... I never thought I'd ever say this: I like the smell of his sweat ..."

"... I'd really like to ask him to give me back all those orgasms I gave him ..."

"... If there was no bad luck, I wouldn't have any luck at all ... "

"... Of course, I kept turning my phone off until I finally realised that no one was calling me any more ..."

"... I dreamed that I was talking to a woman, a psychotherapist, and I was telling her that I always hug my pillow when I sleep. She asked me how long I had been sleeping like that, I pretended I couldn't remember. To myself, I thought: I know, I've been sleeping like that since I got married ... "

" ... Being without all the others made me sad, but being without him makes me tense, that's the fundamental difference ... "

And here I'm beginning to lose the thread. I don't hear them anymore. My ears are completely blocked again, yawning doesn't help, or opening my mouth, or raising my eyebrows. I go back to Victor. I look at the papery cloud in front of me and imagine that it is in fact a ball of cotton wool. Victor is sitting alone in his chemist's shop, it is evening. He breaks off little pieces of that cloud, puts a small white wad of it into each little bottle of medicine and then carefully inserts the stoppers. When he finishes it all, he counts all the bottles again, puts them into the cupboard of remedies and locks it. There is no one there, but those are the rules, medicines have to be locked up. Victor always respects all rules. The best lives have simple rules. Rules bring peace. Peace brings beauty. Victor's life is beautiful. And every ailment has its tablet waiting in the cupboard, to cure it.

Love me tender

1

Elvis smelled fabulous! And his hand did not sweat, despite holding mine in his for two whole minutes. He wrapped his other arm round my waist. Firmly too. Quite firmly. I could feel all of him. The sequins on his high collar tickled my nose a bit. Amazing man, that Elvis! As though he was singing only for me, while we danced. He was whispering, but everyone heard him. OK, he had a microphone, but still.

> *Love me tender, love me sweet,*
> *never let me go ...*

Who would ever want to let you go! You can keep twirling me round like this forever, as far as I'm concerned. Or until we fall into this pool, whatever.

> *You have made my life complete,*
> *and I love you so ...*

I believed every word. And I really wanted to tell him that. But there was no time, and it would not have been right. The man was singing, everyone was watching him, and, which was worse, they were watching me too, and the microphone was there, between my lips and his, which were dramatically close, and who knows what might have transpired in some other situation. And that was just what I wanted to tell him, that I believed everything he said when he was singing. And that he ought to abandon that microphone, flutter his glittering silver cloak and carry me away from here, first down onto the beach, onto the sand, and then who knows where.

Love me tender, love me long, take me to your heart. For it's there that I belong, and we'll never part ...

And as he sang that, as he promised that we would never ever part, Elvis took me back, tenderly, but unambiguously, to my table, swirled his cloak one more time round my head and aimed for the next middle-aged tourist whom he would take for a minute or two, just as he had me, away from her tanned, smiling husband.

That was it. No one was looking at me any longer, all the heads at all the tables round the pool were once again fixed on the false Elvis, although, since I had never danced in the arms of the real Elvis, this was most definitely the most elvis-ish Elvis I had ever felt beside me. It would probably be this one that I would think of from now on when I listened to the real Elvis; that is what I was afraid of.

Elvis was already dancing with a small, stocky German woman who was squeaking somewhere under the level of the microphone, trying to sing a duet with him, but she was too short for that, so that all that could be heard from time to time was a hissing sound, like when you let off a firecracker at New Year. But Elvis covered all that with his sumptuous elvis-ish voice, he did not let it put him off, he twirled the German woman round her two circuits of the pool and then returned her elegantly to her husband.

I was afraid that I might burst into tears. Suddenly. Here, in the middle of my forty-sixth birthday, at the seaside, in the middle of this evening that had started perfectly nicely. What is wrong with me, I thought, if all it takes for me to completely lose my mind is for a pretend Elvis to twirl me twice round a swimming pool? My husband was sipping his drink, with its paper umbrella stuck into its wide-rimmed glass and cheerfully toasted me with it when I returned to the table.

I tried in vain to catch Elvis's eye.

I could not accept it: one moment we had been embracing, here, in front of everyone, he had whispered all those words to me, and the very next moment he would not so much as glance at me. There was no way that Elvis could be like all other men. Elvis must not disappoint me, I felt. Because if even Elvis disappointed me, then what was this whole world coming to?

Just once, swirling past our table, he did glance at me and blew me a kiss. I gulped down my Martini and returned his smile.

2

My husband was already asleep. I was standing on the balcony of our hotel room and looking down at the pool. There was no one at the tables round the pool any more. Just a lad in a neat yellow uniform slowly removing ashtrays, folding table-cloths, closing the remaining umbrellas ...

The water in the pool was almost motionless. Only the moon was reflected in it. And the lights of the surrounding hotels. It was already completely quiet everywhere around. The gardens were closed, the tourists who had wanted to prolong this night had already gone off to some night club or other. Although that seemed a bit unlikely to me. After Elvis, where on earth would you want to go? Apart, perhaps, from ... to Elvis?!

I turned and looked into the room. He was sleeping, soundly. There was no way that he was going to wake up before morning.

Quietly, as quietly as could be, I went into the bathroom and looked at the mirror. Yes, I was forty-six, but I was also tanned and in love. And it is a well-known fact that this makes women suddenly and inexplicably beautiful. I sprayed some scent here and there over myself, more on those places where I was hoping for Elvis than in the places where perfume is usually sprayed, and slipped out of the room with my sandals in my hand. I did not put them on until I was in the lift.

The polite duty receptionist, probably just a few seasons away from retirement, did not at first believe his own ears. However, presumably accustomed to all manner of things in his line of work, he eventually accepted a symbolic banknote, and told me which room Elvis was in. He watched me anxiously as I returned to the lift. I heard him say, more to himself than to me:

'Best of luck, madam!'

3

As though he had been standing right beside the door, Elvis appeared right in front of me the moment I knocked. He was not wearing his cloak or the glittery collar any more, but it was him. No doubt about it. That faultlessly black hair, slicked back, with two or three locks falling onto his brow; those side-burns that reached almost to his lips; the brilliant gleam of his teeth which appeared the instant he saw me. His face was so perfectly tanned that it almost looked like a mask: high cheekbones standing out and those same inimitable lips and smile which pulled slightly to one side. Something between a real smile and a look of contempt.

He was still holding the door handle with his left hand, while his right hand was hovering somewhere in the air, somewhere at the level of his face. It stayed there, almost forming a question mark, as though it were that arm, rather than him, that was asking me who I was, how did he know me and what was I doing here at his door?

We stood like that for a few seconds and it seemed that neither of us was going to speak any time soon. I felt that my mouth had gone suddenly dry and I was a bit breathless. I could hear my own heart in my ears. It was pounding regularly and hard. It got in the way of my thinking. Although, even if I had not heard my heart, who knows whether I would have been thinking anything coherent, then, at that moment. I was simply gazing, and it seemed as though that gazing was going on forever. Because, in those few seconds, I saw every detail that could be seen. Behind Elvis, part of the room was visible: there was a large bed with crumpled sheets, there was also an enormous armchair with tasteless arm-rests in the shape of lions' heads with his sparkling jacket thrown over it. I noticed the dressing table beside the bed and I thought it was amusing that there were little bottles and boxes on it, as though this room belonged to some ancient, powdered lady, rather than to a man. I also saw two suitcases near the door, one huge and green, and a smaller one, with the outline of a silver guitar stuck on it. I saw all of that in those few seconds. And the fact that Elvis's shirt was partly pulled out of his trousers and that he was wearing ordinary checked slippers, just like the ones my husband wore round the house. Those slippers were probably the most extraordinary thing of all.

It was clear that Elvis was not going to say anything soon. That arm was still making a question mark, and all that had changed was that he had raised one eyebrow and slightly turned his neck, lowering his head. That was all. That was his question. I would have to speak; there was nothing else for it.

Softly, so softly that I could hardly hear myself, I said, 'May I come in?'

For a fraction of a second Elvis seemed to hesitate, but then, slowly, moving like a large old tom-cat, he stepped back and let me pass. He still didn't speak. He pointed to the armchair with his jacket thrown over it. It didn't look as though he intended to move it. I slipped past Elvis, feeling his gaze on me the whole time. I picked up the jacket, placed it carefully on the bed and finally sat down.

Elvis was standing beside me. I thought that such things probably happened to him all the time. Women knocking on his door after midnight. He was either too surprised, or not surprised at all. There was no halfway house. That was the first thing I wanted to ask him, but there was no point.

It was only then that I noticed, behind the door, a miniature bar. Elvis moved towards it and when he got there, behind that little counter, he finally spoke,

'You were drinking Martini, if I'm not mistaken?'

My heart leaped. Not only did he remember me, he knew what I had been drinking!

'Yes,' I said, 'thank you, I'd love another Martini.'

Some kind of total calm had come over him. If he had been surprised for the first few moments, it was clear that he had now completely regained control. In one hand he was holding a glass of whisky for himself, in the other my Martini. As he handed me the glass, he said,

'Martini sometimes gives me insomnia, too.'

I almost shouted at him,

'No! It's not the Martini, the insomnia! You ...'

But I could not say any of that. There was a horrible, gigantic, lump in my throat. That same lump that had settled there when I finished my dance with Elvis beside the pool. That humiliating feeling when you know you are going to burst into tears beside a man you do not know at all; and you know that he knows and you know that the tip of your nose has gone red like a very small child's and tears are beginning to well up in the corners of your eyes.

Nothing seemed strange to Elvis. He sat down on the arm of my chair, as though he had mounted one of those lion's heads, stroked my hair and said very gently,

'Oh, my dear! Why, you're really sad ...'

I simply nodded. Just like a child who has given in and decided finally to cry.

Somewhere between his third and fourth whisky, Elvis told me that one night, to his own surprise, he had married a Bulgarian lion tamer. She was a bit wall-eyed, but she was a dab hand with a whip. And he liked that. They only lived together for two years, during which time they mostly quarrelled about whether he should follow the circus or she should follow the Elvis-band, and when they eventually tired of this, they simply went their separate ways. She, to crack her whip and stand tall in front of wide-open jaws, and he to whisper to ladies on the terraces of European resorts.

'You were wise,' I told Elvis. 'People should always follow their dreams. Whatever they are. Marriage is a great killer of dreams.'

'Surely it's not that awful, my dear?'

'No, it's not, it's not awful. But ... it can be a bit dismal. For instance, I catch myself in this kind of thing: he's sitting in his room, working on some stuff of his. I'm sitting in another room, trying, in vain, to concentrate on something. Then I think I might go to him and grab him, at least for a bit, for some kind of sex. He would be up for it. He's always up for it. And I'm just on my way, really, I've already got up, set off towards his room ... But then I glance towards a little table and see that there's a cup there full of steaming cocoa which I've just made –good, warm, sweet cocoa, just the way I like it and – I change my mind. I don't want to let it get cold. I tell myself, OK, I'll drink my cocoa first and then I'll go to his room. But even while I'm thinking that, I already know that nothing will come of it. I know I'm fooling myself. You understand, at that moment I prefer my cocoa to him. And what are you supposed to do then? What?'

Elvis looked at me as though he really understood.

'One night I dreamed about God,' he said. 'God had no form; he was not a human being. He was a kind of creeping plant that wound round a stick or a tree, or something ... Before my eyes, that plant grew and climbed in a spiral up that stick, and in my sleep I knew that this was God who was showing me the meaning of time. I don't know whether I can explain it. That stick in the centre - that was me. The plant was God in transient time. The speed with which the plant grew was the speed with which my life is passing. Something like that ...'

Elvis and I must both have been fairly drunk by now, because it seemed to me that I knew exactly what that climbing plant looked like. I could feel the small white flowers of bindweed growing all over me and wrapping me up. Tender, but merciless tendrils, whose shape adapted to the shape of my body. Little leaves that merged with my skin. I could feel all that here somewhere, at the height of my chest, moving towards my neck and it was only a matter of time before it would wrap round my neck and begin to throttle me.

5

We were floating on the water, both of us. Each on our own lilo. My husband had pulled his peaked cap down over his face, and lay with his arms under his head. The late afternoon sun nuzzled our bodies agreeably. A slight hum from the beach merged with music from three different cafés. And the cries of children. And an old man carefully entering the water, slowly wetting his skin with his hand, bit by bit, as though any speedier action might have cost him his life. Maybe it would, what did I know? And a young couple, not far from us, kissing in each other's arms in the water, and I could only guess that her legs were wound around him, and he was holding her by her arse. For a moment all of that seemed to me perfectly clear. Meanwhile, I was lying motionless and waiting, for something.

I knew exactly what each of those people whom I had already left a little behind me would say at that moment.

And I knew what I would reply.

The climbing plant was still just under my throat, waiting.

I glanced at my husband again. I knew every millimetre of his body. And there was no part of him that I particularly disliked. It was all in some inexplicable way mine, forever. Those fine hairs on his thighs, that youthful fold of his hip, those tended hands, those nipples which for some reason could not tolerate kisses. I knew it all by heart, including what could not be seen, what was lying on the lilo, covered by his swimming trunks; I knew his firmness that sometimes liked to press against me as soon as we woke up, I knew the smell of his breath, and I also knew that in his wildest imaginings he could not guess what I was thinking about just then.

The moment the sun finally disappeared, he felt cool and lifted his cap from his eyes. Squinting a little, he looked at me.

'Shall we go?'

I smiled at him and nodded.

Just today, I told the climbing plant. Just this one day, be patient.

One tenderly green branch, I could see it clearly, had sprouted at just that moment and was waving at me in a cold wind, in front of my eyes, threatening me. Or was it just that night was beginning to fall. I am not entirely sure.

Fairground magician

A vague notion that he would be shagging her that afternoon and the ray of sunlight falling through the window straight onto his keyboard, stroking his fingers, and the heap of wild, crazy words he had never in fact fully expressed while he held her in his arms, they were there somewhere, those words, waiting, like a stopper in a champagne bottle, for someone to draw them out of him, with a pop and a gush, and then those confused memories, like a speeded-up film with a million little images that fly past touching the inside of his thighs, tingling, some such sensation and he was already wriggling at his desk, then he stood up and looked out at the street for a while, a truck was unloading furniture for someone in the next building, he could clearly feel her breasts quivering under his hands, yes, after that she took his two fingers, the two fingers that he had until that moment been pushing into her and she put them in her mouth, she licked them, then he kissed her, deeply, lengthily, and that kiss held the aroma from between her legs, what a kiss that was, for a moment he wondered whether she was kissing him for the last time, but that thought came to him often and it always turned out that he was wrong, thank god, it was just fear, ordinary human fear that anything can be broken, because everything has its end, doesn't it, then he went back to the desk and went on writing to her, my dear, he typed, I have written so many letters in my life and I would like my last one to be to you, however long it is, I don't want to write to where he was already throbbing and she took his hand and placed it on her breasts, his other one felt between her legs, how does she manage to be so wet, always, that's an absolute mystery, and then they talk about all those things, he thinks that he has seen this kind of thing in films, read them in cheap novels, envied, in fact, those non-existent people, thought that such things never happened in real life, anywhere, and here, all of a sudden, it was happening here in the bed where he was waking up, she really was saying those words and he was as well, and it didn't seem at all comical, or sentimental, or cheap, he realises that he has had all of this in him for a long time, is it possible, he wonders, that we all have this in ourselves, this hackneyed take me, take me hard, give yourself to me, give me everything, don't hold anything back, you have to let go, now, now, now, is it possible that we all of us have in us that kitsch animal that dies, sighs, comes with precisely those words, how strange it is, he thinks, I'll never get tired of her orgasms, I'll never get tired of her whimpering in the dark, in the half-dark, in the morning sun, wherever, that moment when she starts to quiver, that moment when I have absolute power over her, when I know clearly that I hold her life in my hands, sometimes I have to make sure, I still my hand, move my tongue away from her, calm my body, and that instant she begins to moan, asking for more, she's just about to come, and that now depends entirely on me, is it possible that all this is simply a game of power, this giving, this taking, am I just pretending to give while really I am taking the sense of power, whatever, whatever, it is quite irresistible, I run my finger over her, how wonderfully she trembles at that, sometimes she lays my hand on a particular place and says here, here, here, and then I give her what she wants there, and then I stop again just to make sure again, and it always works, she always wants more, how often could I do that, he wonders, would a person be able to kill someone like that and why would he do it, are there any cheaper parallels than this, passion and death, sex and death, it's such a cliché, but it really does seem to him that he would be able to kill her like that, if he kept infinitely often interrupting just when she needed it most, he says I want you to beg me, to ask for it, and of course she moans please, please, give it to me, don't stop, that feels so good, I am so stupidly important, she trembles under my hand, under my tongue, she really trembles and really begs me and she's not lying, that's what she's really thinking at that moment, then he asks her will she always be his, yes, yes, she whispers, hardly able to speak, always, truly always, he wants to be sure, yes, yes, always, only go on, and now she settles on him again, clasping him firmly by the shoulders, not letting him lift her off him this time, she rides him, presses her body into him, lowers herself for a moment and allows him to take her nipple between his lips, and then pulls it away, he can clearly feel everything inside her clench, he moves his hips trying to push himself even deeper into her, to reach that place no one has reached before him, and who were all those wankers who screwed her before him, I guarantee they didn't have a clue, there's no way that they would have known how to draw all this out of her, there's no way she would have moaned like this, and writhed, it would be devastating if he realised that she was always like this, it would be terrible if she had asked them all in this same voice to go on doing that, these thoughts came to him and for a moment he felt himself flagging inside her, that helped him, in fact, to wriggle out again and push her onto her back, now she was looking at him a little surprised, a little breathless, her eyes were shining like some crazed junkie's, her pupils were enormous, she had placed her two front teeth over her lower lip as though she was going to bite herself and was looking at him, looking, without saying anything, and he thought that she had looked at others in this same way, perhaps that very day, or the day before, perhaps her husband, who knows, maybe she looked at him like this, you can never tell, we always feel we are entirely unique in someone's life and it always turns out that that was just self-delusion, he sips his tea slowly and now he is fairly certain that he is not going to jerk off, and maybe he won't finish the letter he has begun either, he sees her in his mind sitting at the table opposite him, a long time ago now, when she had almost laughed at him and called him a fairground magician, my husband is a better man than you, she had once said quite seriously and he had seen in her eyes that she really meant it, and what does that mean, for god's sake, what is a better man, how is that measured, does he too want to kill you by flicking his tongue between your legs, does he want to do that, because I certainly do and one day I will, because that's what we do, we fairground magicians, that's our fairground speciality, does he too want to fuck you to death, or does he just want you to take his arm and walk with him to yet another family lunch, in fact I used to be one of those, I listened to my wife's belly where a child was growing, I laid my ear against her belly and watched the brown line which appeared more and more clearly from day to day, I thought that this was how things should be, I

36

really did think that, he went back upstairs and back
to writing to her although she was in the same city, just
a few kilometres away, he says, look at every tree you
pass, look at every leaf on that tree, all of it is telling
you that I love you, I've sent a message through the
plants, through the air, through the insects, birds,
look at the pavement, you will hear it every time your
heel touches the ground, you will hear that same
thing, he writes crazy things although he knows he
will be seeing her probably before she manages to read
this, it doesn't matter, while what he would most like
is to hold her tightly by the neck and push all he has
deep into her, and ask why her husband is a better
man, how come, and in that case why does she keep
coming and letting him to all these things to her, why
do her fingers tremble as she undoes his trousers, why
does she allow him to press her to her knees and force
her to take him in her mouth, why does she ask him to
pull her by the hair, why does she swallow him so
violently if that bloody man is better, he would most
like to choke her like this, he would shove everything
he had down her throat and would not let her go until
they had both drowned under a triple depth, because
he had already thought several times that it was
impossible to reach further than this, and it turned
out that there was something deeper and still deeper,
he felt himself hardening again and began to rub
himself slowly through his trousers, maybe I'll just let
it out a bit, he thought, I won't really wank, just sit
back in the armchair for a while as I wait till the time
comes, and he runs his hand over his balls, feels all the
little hairs on them rise, feels each of his bristling
pores, she always says she likes his balls because they
are heavy and they knock nicely against her bum while

he screws her, he measures the weight of his own balls in his hands and tries to imagine what it's like to be a woman, what it's like when someone enters you, what it's like when you spread your legs and let someone enter you and he almost succeeds, he almost feels a cleft between his legs, it almost seems to him that he is her, and that she is some kind of multi-sexual creature who mounts him and tears him apart, I'm not going to be able not to wank, he thinks, so what, it's such a good feeling, this drawing up and down and up and down, it's almost like being in her mouth, he licks the finger of his other hand and then touches his little head with that finger, imagining that it is her tongue touching him inside there, in her mouth, but her tongue never stops being smooth and moist, while his finger is already dry, he licks it again and puts it back there, while his other hand keeps that rhythm going, how good it would be if she was here, now, at this very moment, if she simply appeared as in some third-rate porn flick and if it turned out that she had no panties and if she would just sit down on me, without many words, without any words, in fact, how I would knock her properly with these balls which she likes, a fairground magician's balls, she would sit here, self-important, full of all those senseless stories about self-control, about how falling in love is a matter of will and personal choice, and then he thought of simply getting up and going away, of giving it all up, but then something else, almost like defiance, you'll whimper, you'll whimper, he thought, you'll beg me for more, and she really did beg him, he stopped for a moment because he felt that, if he were to make any more movements, it would gush out of him, and he didn't want that to happen, he was saving it for her, he had promised that he would save it all for her, and then he thought what, in fact, does it mean when we say I love you, what is contained in those words, what in the end is contained in his I love you, which part of it is this fury and this revenge, which part of it the power she gives him with every sigh, which part is his contest with the one she maintains is a better man than him, what in that I love you remains truly I love you, or does all that together make up love, who would be able to sort it out, who indeed ever dreamed up the myth that love is something perfectly pure, something that cannot be touched, permeated at least, by some blasphemous impulse, and he had told her that possessiveness is a terrible thing and that he would never be like that, that's over, he had said, that finished with the love affairs of my youth, a man loves differently in his fifties, he told her that he used to be crazy and was always afraid that he would lose the one he loved, but with you I am always so serene, with you I'm not afraid, with you I somehow know that you are here and that you will always come back, wherever you go, even when you didn't answer the phone all afternoon, even then I didn't really panic, mind you, I was anxious that something might have happened to you, but I was not afraid for us, I hope that you understand the difference, and that was the greatest of all the lies he had told her, a person is, in fact, always afraid and each new fear is stronger than all his former fears, we never get used to fear or pain, there is just a temporary numbness, an apparent anaesthesia of the senses, a trick that sometimes succeeds, and he really believed this while he was talking to her, but now, here, when he is alone, and when he is holding his erection in his hand, he knows that he has been lying, of course that fear exists, just the same as he had felt when he was twenty, the same as he had felt when one summer that girl went to the other side of the ocean and all he could do was roam around town, more desperate than a lost Bedouin, plot his revenge, plan whether to kill himself or her first and how he was going to do it, truly every new fear is worse than all the previous ones, just as each new passion is stronger, that is presumably why we do things, someone might say that it's because we haven't learned anything, but he thinks it's in fact the opposite, it's because we do learn, it's because we now know exactly how long pain lasts, we know that we will search for her through the streets and that all women will look like her, we know that we will seem to hear her voice under the window and that it will seem to be her car disappearing at the traffic light, and that we will open letters, waiting and waiting, and each time the phone rings we will think that perhaps after all, and so it goes on for years, who would not be afraid of such a curse, but he had told her he was not afraid and that he believed in her so much that it was, in fact, unreal, all other women had brought disquiet, he said, but you bring peace, and he really wanted to believe what he was saying, because he was sick of that disquiet and fear, all right, he thinks, now I can put it back in my pants, I managed not to come, but it was a close shave, my tea is already quite cold, what's the time, quarter past three, another half-hour or so and I can set off, if I go slowly enough, I'll be there at exactly half-past four, and he knows that it will not take him more than fifteen minutes to get there, but he still wants to set off bit earlier, because from the moment he sets off he is in some sense with her, the worst thing is this anticipation of setting off, there is always the all those blankets and woolly hats and covers, you can only see that you are gripping the handle tightly, like a man who has grasped his tiller and believes that he knows where he ought to be going with this little being in front of him, he thinks of all that, as he walks slowly, endeavouring not to get there too early, because he knows that she won't be early, she won't be late either, but she won't come even a minute early, how many minutes have I wasted in my lifetime waiting for women on street corners, in parks, on benches, outside cinemas, at bus stops, with tickets in my hand, in my pocket, with bloody flowers that wilt as I wait, in the sun, in the rain, in the snow, in the wind, how many months of my life, he wonders, would that all add up to, but if we're going to start thinking along those lines, then I ought also to be able to calculate how many minutes I've spent waiting for lifts, and women certainly weren't responsible for that, besides, I like waiting for women who are going to come, and this thought cheers him, I really like waiting for them, especially those I know are going to come, as this one will, and when she appears she will have that expression of hers that doesn't want to hide anything, she hasn't hidden anything for a long time now, she gave herself entirely a long time ago, fairground magician, of course, I'll let her wait for a touch, he plans, I'll let her toss her hair back, push her chest forward, smile, make all those unconscious movements that call me to her and ask, because the longer she waits, the longer she wants, the more fully she will give herself to me later, and she gives herself so well, and all this is because of that, isn't it, all of this is just because of that moment, a whole life reduced to that one thing, the moment of someone's surrender, everything else is an overture to that, everything else is just setting the scene, framing, making the frame for that one picture, here I am, fifteen minutes early, he's a little cross with himself, but not much, his glance keeps flying to the corner round which her car will appear, but not yet, not for at least another quarter of an hour, but he still keeps looking and doesn't manage to look for long at the other things around him, the trees that have in the meantime blossomed while they were kissing in hidden places, another ten minutes, he puts on his slightly surly expression that he'll be able to maintain until their first kiss, until he smells the perfume that always reminds him of the scent of apples, until he hears her first sigh and then he will be flooded once again with his own power over her, and his power paradoxically makes him generous, he calls her his slave while he kisses her and tells her that she is the only slave who can lord it over him and choose whatever she likes, but that doesn't make her less of a slave, because her power does not exist in itself, it exists only because he bequeaths it to her, those are the sort of crazy things he tells her and she looks at him quite seriously and says that's what I've always wanted, I've always dreamed about being someone's slave, but nobody was able to do that, nobody knew how to draw that out of me, he raises her arms high and presses them against the wall and holds her like that for a few moments, as though nailing her to it, she doesn't even try to move, calm, meek, as though she really does belong only to him, as though she does not move around every day among other people, as though she spends her whole life just sitting behind closed windows, waiting for him to come, you are a wonderful archetype, he thinks as he bends her arms behind her back, not wanting to say that out loud because a word like that has no place in sex, but in some strange way it arouses him, you are the archetype of everything that a woman ought to be and you are that precisely because I know how to stimulate you, you were never that before, you were never that for the others, admit that you weren't, she shrieks in his thoughts and he bends her arm more firmly against her back, but she doesn't hear his thoughts, just feels that he is drawing her further and further down, and then she falls on her knees in front of him, once again, like every time, and wraps her arms round his legs, pulls his trousers down, turns him, licks the inside of his knees, does everything to please him, to calm the anger whose cause he does not even attempt to hide from her, there is always some reason for his archetype to be furious with her archetype, she feels that instinctively, and runs her warm tongue over his thighs, soothing it all, the anger, fear, pain, all that lost time, really what time is it, another three minutes, she'll be here any minute, he stares in that direction, one car, another, a third, no, no, no, it's not this one either, or the next, where is she, for god's sake, he feels that stirring in his trousers again, I'll shag her, I'll soon be shagging her, it's not this one either, she'll just appear suddenly, he'll recognize the little red roof turning swiftly and he'll know that she can already see him, because he always waits for her here, in the same place, is she thinking about that as she comes towards him, he wonders, is she already trembling inside, and he knows that he will soon be asking her, and that she will tell him at exactly which corner she began to drip, no, she will not be lying, just as she was not lying when she begged him not to stop, she will park beside him, glance at him through the glass, to someone passing by that glance would mean nothing, but he knows exactly, she will open the door, first one leg will emerge, then the other, his eyes always slip along those calves where he has so often run his tongue and lips, then back to her face, to her eyes which are still waiting for him to look at her, and he will watch as she gets out and locks the door and then when she will be standing next to him, not saying anything, simply waiting, for him, the fairground magician, to sweep her off, no matter where, that is why he gazes in that direction almost without blinking, waiting for her like his prey, with which he will feed himself, compressing this waiting into himself, drop by drop, barb by barb, counting, pulsating, feeling the afternoon sun on the back of his neck, transforming himself into an arrow with a poisonous, deadly tip that is just about to fly, talking slowly to himself, stretching that bow taught silently in himself, he holds his breath, looking in that same direction, to that same corner where at any moment something that has to come will appear.

Zugzwang

1

There is a situation in chess usually known by the German word 'Zugzwang'. It means that you are in a cleft or, more precisely, 'a squeeze'. There is an aggressor and there is a victim and usually the latter is obliged to make a move that will inevitably lead him to lose the game. The rule is simple: it is your move, and you have to play, and the fact that you will put yourself at a disadvantage – is your problem.

2

That night as well, it all began with operatic arias. She had already begun at least partially to grasp the order of things. First soft music. Then slightly louder music. Then very loud music mixed with sobs that at times drowned out the loudest sopranos. Then the music stopped, but the sobs remained, half human, half animal. And after it all, silence.

Half her face is leaning against the wall. Helena is trying to hear. The noise from the street sometimes means that she loses the thread, but then it all comes back. She hears them singing that strange song. She cannot make out the words, but the rhythm is already familiar. The same thing happens almost every night. It makes her flesh creep, but she does not stir from the wall. She is cold. It is a bit like a kind of prayer. Or the combined baying of wolves. Or birth scenes in films. 'Oh, no, no, no, no ...'

sometimes breaks through everything else, but then the harmonious voices above it all. The floor is cold. She puts a cushion under her knees, on the floor, and wraps a shawl round herself. It is summer, she should not be cold. The cold is coming from over there, from the other side of the wall.

When the neighbours moved in, Helena watched through the spy hole in her front door. It was a quiet arrival, almost unnoticed. Everything was very well organised. A few workers carried the furniture in as discreetly as possible. All the pieces were carefully wrapped. Or packed in boxes. The sounds from the other side of the wall began two days later.

3

She had turned off the telephone ring tone, but every few minutes she heard the answer-phone click. She put the cushion over her head; she did not want to hear the messages. They were all the same. But she could still hear, despite the cushion. She heard Martin, her now ex-lover, saying the same thing over and over again: 'This doesn't make sense. This is torture. Be sensible.' Or else he said: 'There's no way you can drive me away.' She goes and unplugs the telephone. An unusual silence. Part of her mind expects the answer-phone to come on again, despite it all being unplugged. But nothing happens. And she finds that unbearable. After a few minutes, she plugs the telephone in again, stands beside it and waits, waits, waits, until she hears that 'click' and 'beep' and then his voice. All over again. She puts the cushion back over her head.

Everything connected with Martin had been predictable, from the first moment. The way he put his jacket down, the way he placed a bottle of wine on the table, his uncertainty about where he should sit and immediately afterwards his excessive relaxation in a space that was new to him. This man exists to kill mystery, she had thought that first day, but he was there, he was always there and quite definite. And at her age, a man who was definite acquired additional value for just that reason. Still, shards of fear from some buried time would sometimes crash onto the floor and no one would hear, apart from her. She would shiver. He would go on sleeping.

4

At twilight, her sister arrived. In a fluttering dress made of something more like gauze than anything a dress should be made of. You could see her thin legs and boyish hips.

'It's unbearably hot outside,' said her sister. 'Is your air-conditioning still not working?'

'There's no point getting it fixed if I'm moving soon. And I will move, for sure.'

Sandra, the only member of the family she still saw, shot her that lengthy, penetrating glance so like their mother's. She would raise her left eyebrow, and the right end of her lip would curl oddly into something that was half a smile and half disappointment. Something like that.

'Where are you going this time?' Sandra asked finally.

'Not far enough, probably.'

Sandra just waved her hand, ineptly pretending this was of no interest at all to her. Although Helena knew that she would bring it up again, sooner or later. When, where, why, for how long ...

'Any news of your mysterious neighbours?' asked Sandra.

Helena put a bowl of peanuts and a large glass of vodka with ice on the floor beside her.

'I think someone's shut up in there. I think very strange things are going on there. *Rosemary's Baby*, something like that. I wouldn't be surprised if there was a secret door into their apartment through my wardrobe.

Sandra leapt up delightedly,

'Let's go and check!'

And she had already taken everything out of the wardrobe and flung it onto the bed. Helena went on drinking her vodka, powerless to stop her. She knew that Sandra would not be putting it all back into the wardrobe, she would have to do it all herself. She took everything out, even the empty suitcases from the top shelf. Then she climbed onto a chair and investigated every corner of the wardrobe. She tapped a few times, then listened, seriously and professionally, as though she had discovered secret partitions countless times. At one moment it seemed to both of them that someone on the other side of the wardrobe was responding to Sandra's tapping on its back with the same *tap, tap, tap,* but then they fell silent, and started giggling, and nothing else happened. They tapped a few more times, but there was no further response. It did not happen again. They were already too much under the influence of the vodka to know for certain whether someone had tapped from the other side or not.

Some hours later, the two of them were lying on the large bed. There were still clothes from Helena's wardrobe tossed all around them. The vodka bottle on the floor was empty. Only the constant noise of the town could be heard in the distance.

'Are you asleep, Helena?'

Silence. Helena could not be bothered to reply.

'Or are you dead?' added Sandra.

'I think I'm dead,' said Helena softly.

'So? How're things there?'

'Imagine you're lying on the pavement of the busiest street. Are you doing that?'

'Yes. Carry on.'

'You're lying on the pavement and watching everything from down there. Your arms are spread out. Your legs are spread out. Nothing rubs and your back isn't cold, even though you're lying on asphalt. You don't feel anything. You see thousands of people passing by you, over you and everywhere around. You see all of them, but they don't see you. Some of them cross straight over your body, but their soles and high heels don't hurt you. You just know that at a certain moment they have stepped on you. You feel it like a slight tickle in your nose. Then you forget the people and look at the sky. You slow down the birds' flight with your eyes. If you concentrate really hard, you can raise yourself up. Roughly to the eighth floor. And hover there.'

'Only the eighth?'

'I don't want to go higher than that; people are too

small when I look at them from above.'

'Does that mean that at that height you sometimes turn over and look down?'

'No, it's not quite like that. It's rather that I've got eyes everywhere, all over my body.'

'You know what, Helena?'

'What?'

'You've been smoking pot. Admit it. You were smoking while I was asleep.'

'I admit it.'

'Super. You're a selfish sister. You smoke pot and you don't share it with me.'

'Sandra, what do you say to going to my neighbours and asking what it is I can hear from their apartment every night?'

Sandra said nothing for a while. Pretending to be thinking it over. As though she was ever in any doubt about anything.

'You realise that this is one of *those* ideas?' asked Sandra.

'Aha!'

As they left the apartment, giggling and on tiptoe, as in a conspiracy, Helena happened to notice the digital clock in the hall out of the corner of her eye. It was one sixteen a.m. That made everything seem all the funnier.

6

Even outside the door, they could hear the music. And someone's footsteps. At the same moment, Helena rang the doorbell, and Sandra knocked. Which forced them to stifle another giggle.

They did not notice that the door had been

opened. Without a sound. Only suddenly the man with long greying hair, drawn into a pony-tail, looking a bit like a Native American, was standing in front of them. Not in the least surprised.

'Ah, so here you are at last,' said the man, looking at Helena.

He gestured for them to come in.

'This is my sister, Sandra, and I'm Helena.'

'I know, of course. You're both welcome, you can change behind that screen, everything you need is there. As soon as you're ready, I'll introduce you to Magda. She'll be pleased to know that you're here ...'

There was no space for them to say anything. They were just vaguely aware of the fact that they had stopped giggling and gone obediently behind a large, exotic screen, with paintings on it of flaming red birds with long necks. Are they flamingos, Helena wondered, but she did not say anything out loud. It seemed pointless to say anything at all.

And there, behind the screen, on a wide plush stool, two transparent, incredibly light dresses were waiting. They put them on in silence, as though automatically, incapable of thinking what was going on. They dressed to the rhythm of the music that was getting steadily louder.

'I'm waiting,' they heard his voice from the other side of the screen.

And they came out, with their obedient faces. Aware that their bodies were almost completely visible through the material. Aware that their breasts swung softly as they walked.

'Follow me,' said the man. 'Now you're going to meet Magda. You may speak only when she asks you something, or when I give you permission, I hope you understand?'

The girls nodded.

The room they entered was in half-darkness. Their eyes took a second or two to get used to it, and then, in the darkest corner, where there was a large, imposing bed with four substantial wooden columns and a canopy. In the middle of the bed, they could see the tiny, barely perceptible body of a woman. She looked so small that she made just a slight hump in the cover. The woman was covered up to her breasts; her arms were lying calmly by her sides. One could see the delicate collar of her nightgown and her thin, withered neck, emerging from that collar. Her sunken eyes had once been unbelievably beautiful and bright. Now they just shone with a sickly, deathly glow.

The man looked at the two of them as though ensuring that every detail on them looked as it should.

'This is Magda.' Then, turning towards the woman, he went on, 'My dear, here are Helena and Sandra. They're going to keep us company tonight. I'm sure they'll be wonderful company, won't they?'

'Wonderful, yes. Wonderful company ...'

Magda's voice was quiet, barely audible. As though it was already coming from the other side. As though it already contained its own echo. It was not possible to judge rationally how old Magda was. The skin of her arms looked young. But her face bore centuries in itself. Very dark rings drew her eyes inwards. Burning. With an effort, Magda raised her left hand and pointed towards them as though signalling for them to start. Glancing at the girls, she said:

'Have you got drinks?'

'Oh, how forgetful of me,' cried the man. 'I forgot to offer our visitors a drink! I'll be with you immediately, just give me a minute. Stay here, with Magda, while I prepare your cocktails.'

And he left the room, silently.

Helena and Sandra stood there, at the foot of the bed, looking at Magda. Not saying a word.

It seemed that every word she spoke cost her a great effort. First she would quietly clear her throat, and then, slowly, as though afraid that her words would disappear somewhere between her and the person she was speaking to, she began to talk.

'Don't be afraid and don't worry. Wherever I go out of this room, I shall take you with me, in my heart. All bodies are one body. All bodies can come together, if that is what we wish. That's a secret that no one has divulged to you, isn't it?'

The girls glanced at each other. They did not know whether this was a question or simply a statement. They shook their heads. No, no one had told them that before.

'Love sometimes has an ugly face,' Magda went on. 'But its soul is always in a state of perfection.'

At that moment the man appeared, carrying two glasses.

'Your cocktails. They are to be drunk headlong and without hesitation.'

They smelled the scent of aniseed and traces of nutmeg, and that was all. In an instant the world became light. Their fear vanished. Everything vanished. All that remained was the desire to go on and to plunge into this night. Headlong and without hesitation, just as the man had said.

He led their obedient bodies. Sandra took

hold of one column of the bed, Helena another. Their hands were high above their heads.

'These columns are your perfect lovers,' whispered the man. 'You can feel their warmth in your hands. Show them how much you desire them. Abandon yourselves to them.'

Helena and Sandra felt the bulges and hollows of those columns, which had suddenly come alive and they could have sworn that pure love was pulsating out of them. Magda's eyes flew from one girl to the other. The man's hands were everywhere. They guided their own hands, they passed lengthily and slowly from their knees to their hair. He whispered to them and led them into that mysterious space.

'Helena, don't take your hands off the column. Feel how much it loves you. Press against it, Sandra, it wants you to wrap your legs round it, it wants you to slide over it like an amorous snail. Your hands can set this bed on fire. Your bodies can set the world on fire. Feel free to run your tongues over the columns, give them all your juices, smell their taste. Give yourselves to them.'

Magda's eyes were burning, burning. They trembled as her arms on the cover did. Magda had been right, all the bodies of the world can merge into one. His hands passed from one to the other, they were all over them, it was all becoming one, logical, trembling, hot body. The music was getting louder, their breaths ever faster. Their columns opened themselves up to them and loved them as no one had ever loved them before. He embraced them as they had never thought anyone could. Their columns had velvet skin and the scent of pure desire. They stood there, and their legs wrapped further and further around the columns, the space between them drawing them ever closer towards them. They would never know whether those were the man's hands, or had they sprung somewhere out of those columns, touching them so that their stomachs trembled in a wild rhythm.

At a certain moment, Magda just said softly: 'Darling ...'

And the man went slowly over to her, lifted up the cover, under which could be seen no more than forty dying kilograms. He lifted her nightgown, slowly, carefully separated her legs, evidently paralysed, and lay down on Magda, still whispering:

'Girls, this is the moment for you to send great love towards this bed. I want you to touch yourselves where you are hottest, I want to feel you trembling, I want your passion here in myself, come on, come on, Magda will accept you in her mind if you send her enough love, orgasm is in your mind, my darling Magda, orgasm comes from your mind, and not from between your legs, take me, come on, merge with us, my love ...'

The world trembled along with them. The world collapsed under them. Orgasm came from who knows whose brain and flung itself over their bodies like the crazed broken cable of a high-tension wire ...

7

Sandra was the first to wake. She glanced around. She realised that she was in Helena's apartment and that she was lying curled up in the big, comfortable armchair. Helena was lying on her stomach on the bed. She was slowly waking up as well. She raised her head, caught sight of Sandra in the armchair, covered her eyes with one hand as though the daylight bothered her and finally spoke:

'Heavens! What a sick dream I had!'

Sandra checked whether she was able to move her legs. She could. But not in an altogether coordinated way. She would need a bit of time for that, she knew.

'I had a strange dream as well,' said Sandra.

'It can't be as crazy as mine, no way.'

'Helena, I think we both had the same dream. That happened once when we were small, do you remember?'

'So what did you dream about?' Helena sat up, as though suddenly wide awake.

'Magda, just like you,' said Sandra calmly.

They just looked at one another and knew that they would never mention this dream again, just like the first one. In that distant dream, they had been little girls, their father came into their room, it was night, they were asleep, their father lifted up their covers, their nightdresses, parted their thin, children's legs and then touched them tenderly, very tenderly, saying in a soothing tone *sssshhhh, daddy loves you, daddy loves you very much.*

The following day, when their father had gone to work, Sandra was eating her breakfast silently, while Helena told their mother the dream they had both had. Their mother's hands grasped the edge of the table for a few seconds, and then she stood up abruptly, snatched the plates from in front of them, looked at her daughters in a way they had never seen before, crossed herself and said:

'Preserve me, Lord, from the demon in this child! To imagine such things! You ought to be ashamed, Helena!'

For Helena, all the years that followed after that were just waiting to leave; to go as far away as possible, to disappear forever.

8

The telephone rang. And the answer machine clicked on again. They waited for a few moments and then Martin spoke out of the machine, in a slightly metallic voice,

'I don't know what to say to you any more, Helena. You know that I love you, you do, don't you?'

And he paused, but his breath told them he was still there, by his receiver. Helena leapt up, grabbed the telephone and said,

'Is that you, Martin?'

He said nothing for a moment or two, not believing his ears, and then, almost breathlessly, he said,

'Yes, it's me. Helena, what is it ...'

'Nothing, don't say anything. Just come. I have to tell you something wonderful.'

'Are you sure?'

'Yes, Martin, I'm quite sure. And, you know what?'

'What?'

'I love you too ... Everything will be fine from now on ... Everything ... You'll see ... Martin, love sometimes has an ugly face, but its soul is always in a state of perfection.'

'I'm on my way,' said Martin hastily and the connection was lost.

Sandra gathered her things from the floor, in silence. It was time for her to leave. Helena scooped her hair up cheerfully into a grip, threw off her clothes and went to take a shower. The sky was clear. There was not a single cloud to be seen.

Aurora Borealis

1

'Hello? Did I wake you?'

'Mmm ... No.'

'Why don't you ever want to admit you were asleep? I can see from your voice that you've just this moment woken up.'

'See? From my voice?'

'OK, *hear* from your voice. Why do you keep picking me up on little errors?'

He felt comfortable in his afternoon grumpiness. All too often he felt he was like an excited cocker spaniel ready to wag its tail for hours just because someone had stroked its ears in passing. Grumpiness was better. It left him more space for dignity.

'Listen,' he said, 'forget that now. Come over and make us a decent cup of coffee. OK?'

Katja wriggled by the telephone; he could hear her.

'I don't want to have coffee with you, really. I just called to see how you are.'

'You're worried about me?'

'Don't be cynical. I don't want anything to happen to you. I don't want you to lose it completely. I don't want you to spend the rest of your life in pyjamas, behind closed blinds.'

'How do you know there's such a thing as the rest of my life?'

'I hope there is,' she said, after a short pause. 'I hope

that there will be a continuation of your life and a continuation of my life. I hope that that continuation will make some sense.'

He looked around him, without any particular aim and suddenly realised that his foot under the table was kicking a small soft object. He wanted to bend down and find out what it was, but at the same time he knew it was better not to do that. The soft objects that kept on appearing in odd corners of the house caused him pain.

'Are you there, Oliver?'

Katja's voice came from some other life, a life in which it had not happened that his bare foot had tossed off its slipper and set off fearfully to feel around it. I shall know you at the first touch, thought Oliver. As soon as my foot touches you, I shall know what you are.

His big toe touched a soft ear. A cold plastic eye. Then the braces of the trousers that plush rabbit had on. He recognised it at once. That is what it was: the rabbit with the red trousers and braces. On the front, where the braces were hooked, the word BOOM was written in large yellow letters. He did not need to look down to know all that.

'I'm here,' said Oliver.

'Why aren't you saying anything?'

'I've found the rabbit under the table. That one with the trousers and braces.'

He heard only her very soft sigh.

Then they said nothing for a few moments. Finally, she spoke again,

'You really must get rid of all that stuff once and for all. You simply must.'

'There's nothing I must do. Nothing.'

His voice was lost in that whispered *nothing, nothing, nothing* and then she just heard him put down the receiver.

2

With his foot still stroking the plush rabbit under the table, with his elbows on the table, he tried to think what would be more sensible: to have a shower or make a coffee. The coffee was essential to give him the energy for a shower, but equally, a shower was an essential precondition for making coffee. How can I decide, he wondered. What if I never decide and stay forever at the table, immobilised by my dilemma? What if I never do summon up the energy to do either of these two things? Then he thought that it wasn't all that important, after all. He had already made all the important wrong decisions. He had made them with incredible ease. With an absolute lack of awareness that every detail, even the slightest, had its own weight. We're not going fishing today, he had said to the boy, one ordinary morning, nearly three years ago. We'll go tomorrow. I've still got a lot to do today. The boy had started to cry. His big brown eyes looked even larger when they were full of tears like that. His eyelashes shone. He thought: my son has eyelashes like a girl's. He did not console him. He believed that you should not console boys too much. He let him stand for a while, crying like that, with the fishing rods in his hand. The rods were far bigger than him; he always looked comical when he was carrying them. He told the boy to stop crying and put the rods back in the cupboard. Someone would trip over them, he said.

The boy glanced at him once more, blinked those wet lashes a few times, and then turned away. Oliver heard the boy opening the cupboard, putting the rods back, jumping up to take his blow-up ball from the shelf and then go outside.

Decisions like those. Quite unimportant. Decisions I make every day, thought Oliver. Decisions that make life just that bit more agreeable.

This business with the rabbit under the bed reminded him of a game that he and Katja had once liked to play in bed, in the days when things made some sense. He would lie on his back, his eyes closed, and she would place individual items on his foot. He had to guess what they were. Some of the things were quite small and he could hold them between two of his toes, and then use the other foot to examine them carefully. That's a Hungarian die, he would cry. Those are nose-drops. A lighter? Is this a lighter? Ah, this is a little packet … Cigarettes? Nooo … a cassette? This is something cold and round. Is it a clock? A mobile phone?

They could play like that for hours, while the boy slept in the other room. And then one morning, everything began to look different. Make me a coffee, love. Would you like to bath him today? Might he have a temperature, his cheeks are a bit red? What'll we eat tonight? You know that I can't take yoghurt before going to sleep, the acid will bother me. Put another blanket over me, please. I think there's something knocking in the engine, could you have a look. That whole repertoire. Everything had vanished in an instant.

3

For the last three years, strangers in bars had been the people Oliver talked to most. He would usually start by suddenly asking them some quite ordinary question. People in bars were not used to other people asking them why their tie was tied so tightly, what did they think about the fact that there were many more women in the world than men, had they ever wanted to kill anyone and what had stopped them, had they ever dreamed anything under anaesthetic, how did they see themselves in ten years' time, what would they like to be in their future lives, what did they feel when they saw a pool of blood, had they ever had to kill an animal, where did they put their unspoken fury, were they hoping for anything, and so on ... Oliver had never been afraid of silence between sentences. He let the people consider his questions. He did not insist on looking his collocutors in the eye. He would let them gaze somewhere over there, behind the bar, and really give some thought to why hundreds of dolphins had suddenly beached on some coast in New Zealand. Had they decided to commit collective suicide? Had they been driven there by a gigantic underwater wave? Or a sea monster? Do dolphins perhaps know something we do not and is the fact that we do not know all that is saving us from committing collective suicide ourselves? And what, finally, do they think about the people who put the dolphins back in the water, depriving them of the right to decide about their own life and death? What do they think about the people who believe that they know better than the dolphins what is the right thing to do? What would you do if you saw a beached dolphin, he asked the people. And on the whole people thought that beaching was an accident and not a matter of choice. Yes, but hundreds of dolphins, Oliver would insist. At that, the people would usually shrug their shoulders, not believing that such a thing was possible. If it did happen, it happened in some place that was so far away from them that it did not merit their consideration. Far away? Really far away? What is a safe distance, Oliver would keep on, but by that time the person he was talking to would usually get up and move to some other place in the bar. And since Oliver would not follow them, that other place would indeed seem to be just that; a safe distance.

4

He left the bar and set off down the street, with his hands in his coat pockets. Oliver remembered how much he had once hated this November wind, in the days when he could still hate and love. Now he just put his hands in his pockets and registered that it was blowing. There was a girl standing in the street, turning to her left and right, as though expecting something. She's looking for a taxi, thought Oliver. Or maybe he did not think it; maybe he said it out loud? Because the girl turned to him and said,

'Yes, taxis come down this street so rarely, I don't know why...'

'I can take you, my car's just here,' said Oliver.

The girl looked at him in a slightly different way. It would help if I smiled now, thought Oliver. But he no longer smiled. And so he didn't smile at this girl either. He just stood beside her, letting her assess for herself whether he was a serial killer, an importunate seducer or simply a concerned citizen. He stood, looking at the tips of his shoes.

Whether because there was no kind of smile, or because he did not pronounce a single additional sentence to try to persuade her to go with him, after just a few seconds' thought, the girl suddenly made her decision,

'Okay. I hope that your car is nearby.'

'It is,' said Oliver, 'you're leaning on it.'

She said her name was Marina. Good, thought Oliver, I'll do my best to forget that quickly. People's names carried in them something too personal. Behind the names, there were usually life stories, stories about other people in those lives, stories about hopes, disappointments, and mistakes. Oliver could no longer listen to stories about other people's mistakes. Still less about other people's successes. Sometimes he felt that all he could do was stare at other people or curl up against someone's body for an instant, just to convince himself that he was still alive. And that was all.

Half an hour later, he was sitting in Marina's apartment, drinking brandy. He tried not to look around. Just like people's names; objects were too personal. Someone's books. Music that someone liked. Photographs. The choice of objects and colours in the apartment. All that expressed things that Oliver did not want to know.

And that is why over the last few years he had cultivated a way of looking between half-lowered eyelashes. Whenever there was something near him that he did not want to see, he imagined that he was looking at his own eyelids, from inside. The first time he had looked at the inside of his eyelids, he remembered, was that night in the hospital. Katja was sitting beside him, her lips as pale as the wall, her eyes fixed, without blinking, on the boy who was lying unconscious, wired up to machines, and at a certain moment Oliver realised that he could no longer see any of that. He looked, but he no longer saw. There was just that play of colours on the inside of his eyelids. Concentric circles that merged into each other. Waves of colours that came from nowhere and danced in front of his open eyes. If he just shifted his lashes a fraction, those waves would ripple in quite a different way. The most unusual shapes would surface out of those waves. Strange human forms would appear. Animals. Exotic trees. A gigantic baobab. The outlines of naked bodies swaying. And always in the end, he would return to the waves. It was a pure, perfect beauty that he saw that night for the first time. And about which he could never speak to Katja. He would not dare to. She squeezed his hand, there beside the boy who was quite obviously dying, and all that Oliver was able to think about then was the explosion of colours on the inside of his own eyelids. Everything vanished before that miracle. Things disappeared. His own personal aurora borealis was born that night, and never left him. Just as he did not leave it.

So he watched, hazily, through his own eyelashes, playing with his own inner shadows, while that girl (Marina?) put on a CD and talked about a concert that she had nearly gone to and then something had happened ...

Here the thread was broken. The thread always broke for Oliver wherever he wanted. Sounds remained, but no sense. And the sound of her voice was pleasant. In itself, a fine, not unduly loud, melody. Not overly shrill, but not too low either. Just what he liked. The tone of her voice went well with the taste of the brandy.

'I presume you're married?' said the girl, more like a statement of fact, but with the intonation of a question.

This gave him a jolt. It almost woke him.

'No,' said Oliver. 'I'm not.'

'Really?'

The girl was genuinely surprised.

'Really. One night my ex-wife dreamed an unusual dream and after that she no longer wanted to be my wife.'

'Do I want to hear that dream?'

'I don't know whether you have a choice,' said Oliver, realising that this was another moment when most people would have smiled.

'All right,' she said, lighting a cigarette. 'I'm listening.'

'In that dream, my ex-wife goes into our bathroom and sees that the little plate covering the drain on the floor has moved. She calls me to come and fix the plate. I come in and put it back. But at that moment, when I move the plate, the toilet bowl falls through the floor and down into the cellar. It does not fall right to the floor of the cellar, mind, but remains hanging by a wire, which is far more terrible...

'By a thread...' interjected Marina.

'Quite, it's hanging by a thread, somewhere down there over the cellar. And Katja bends down, kneels in fact, and looks down, through the hole in the bathroom floor. Completely horrified. And as she's looking down like that, suddenly her wedding-ring slips off and disappears somewhere down there in the cellar. The ring is followed by the keys to the apartment; they must have fallen out of her pocket, or something. Now Katja is completely desperate. There is a hole in the bathroom floor and she has lost her wedding ring and the keys of the apartment. Then she tells me to go down into the cellar and find her things. And I go down. She can see me from our bathroom searching through the cellar, but I don't manage to find any of the things. She calls to me from up there, telling me where to look, but that doesn't help. I go back to the apartment and tell Katja that I haven't found her ring or the keys. She says, "He's completely incompetent; I'll have to go down and find them myself." And that's the end of her dream.'

Marina was silent for a while. Then she said,

'She didn't altogether want to leave you. She thought she would be able to find a solution.'

'I know, that's how it looks in the dream. But, in reality, it seems that she hasn't found everything she lost either.'

'Have you any idea why you couldn't find the lost things in her dream?'

'Who knows,' said Oliver. 'Things disappear. Sometimes they disappear forever. Sometimes they get stuck in invisible cracks. Sometimes they are in front of our noses, but we still can't see them. Or... Or I really was incompetent, as Katja thought in her dream. That's the most likely explanation.'

Oliver knew where this kind of conversation led. And he knew that Marina knew too. That was his way. And this could not remotely be called a tactic, because it was a very long time since Oliver had had any tactics. He would just say what he really thought and something about his manner made women come up to him and put their arms round him.

5

He had his evening rituals now. Slow, pointless walks beside the river, past the barges that were for the most part shut up and dark at this time of year. Just here, in the place where he was now standing, one distant year, Katja and he had seen a flock of swans on a January night. They were gliding over the water and making loud calls. It was impossible to know whether the swans had just landed there to rest, whether they lived there, among the barges, or were simply lost. Katja and he stood for a while watching them. He held Katja's hand in his, trying to warm it. There was no one there apart from themselves and the swans.

That might have happened in some previous life, thought Oliver. The water was now still and dark and there was no sound. In that previous life, which no longer existed anywhere apart from in his memory, after their walk Katja and he had returned to the parking space and got into the car. Their breath misted the glass and for a few minutes they were protected from outside glances.

'Swans on a January night,' said Oliver. 'Isn't that truly miraculous?'

Katja looked at him.

'Of course,' she smiled at him. 'Only people don't usually recognise miraculous things, when they're happening.'

In this present life, Oliver felt that it was only now that he had become aware of the meaning of that distant miracle.

He decided to call her and tell her. His fingers were frozen, he blew on them beside the river and thought that he would not be able to key in Katja's number, but then, all at once, there was her voice and he said simply,

'Do you remember those swans?'

'Of course,' said Katja, as though there was nothing unusual in being phoned late at night and asked such a question.

'What do you think, were they cold?'

'Very. Even then I was convinced that they had landed there just to show us something.'

'Yes ... But what?'

'Presumably to show us that sometimes beauty is possible only where one least expects it.'

'And what, if anything, did you and I learn from that? What was the point of it all? What have I gained from once having seen fucking swans on the river and been aware of beauty? What have I gained apart from now knowing that it can never be repeated? Not in this life, certainly ...'

Katja sighed, fell silent for a while and then said,

'You're there now, aren't you?'

'What's that got to do with anything ...?'

'Why don't you come over here? We'll make some tea and have a chat.'

'And be happy ever after?'

'Don't be cynical. You don't have an exclusive right to pain.'

'No. That's right. But I have never said that I wanted to be happy again. And you did say that you did.'

'I said that I did. But I never said I had succeeded.'

'But what does it mean to be happy, Katja, what does it mean? Do you really think it's possible ever again? And why should that have to be what I want? How do you do it, Katja? You wake up in the morning and tell yourself: I'm going to be happy today. It doesn't matter that everything has fallen apart, it doesn't matter that my son is dead, it doesn't matter that I watched his arms growing ghostly thin in just a few days, it doesn't matter that none of that needed to happen, if, say, that truck had set off just a minute earlier or a minute later; none of that matters, what matters is for me to be happy again, because, heaven knows happiness is the most important thing in the world! Is that how it's done, Katja? Teach me, you know all these things about happiness!'

'This is cruel. You yourself know it's cruel. Don't talk like that.'

He could hear her voice beginning to waver, as though she was just about to start crying.

'And who should I talk to about these things? I'm a man who still wonders every day whether there is any point in breathing in air, and you left me because I refused to be happy!'

He realised that he was almost yelling, here beside the river.

Katja listened. She always listened, no matter how much he talked. And however loudly he spoke. Or quietly. Or through his tears. There was something good in that, but he did not know exactly what. He could always shout at her and for as long as he had to, Katja never said that she did not want to go on listening to him. There was something good in the fact that Katja was infinitely prepared to let him blame her. She took this rage on herself just as steadfastly as she had once taken his body into her. There was no end to it. He had known that then, and he knew it now. But, again, it turned out that there had been an end after all. Did that mean that this would stop at some point? He had never asked Katja that, ever. He would never admit such a thought to her.

'Katja,' he said again, 'do you really want to be happy again?'

'I don't see that you are doing anything cleverer than that.'

'I can't understand you. I'll be damned if I can understand that.'

'So? What are we going to do about it, now? It's a sin that you will never forgive me, is that it? What's more terrible, the fact that you don't understand me or that I want to feel, just once, perhaps, that I'm alive again and that the fact that I'm alive makes some sense?'

'I don't know. In any case, I just wanted to tell you that, about the swans.'

'What did you tell me, exactly?'

'Why that, that I knew they were cold. Like me now.'

'Oliver ...'

But he had already ended the call.

6

He had told the boy to go outside and play. They'd go fishing the next day, he said. The boy brushed his tears away with his sleeve. His right sleeve. The blue striped sweatshirt they had bought him on the third floor of the department store, that same spring, just a few days earlier. He saw himself taking that shirt out of the pile, unfolding it in front of the boy, laying it against his shoulders, assessing the size and then saying,

'This'll be just right.'

The boy had nodded. He liked new things.

'It'll be just right,' he said. 'Let's get it.'

The boy takes the ball and goes outside.

Oliver goes into the living room and glances at the pile of accounts waiting for him on the table. He turns on the computer. His thoughts are perfectly clear. As clear as they can sometimes be on a Saturday morning.

He opens the first document. He checks the figures. He glances at the paper. Compares them. Everything matches. He checks again. Then he opens the second document. Checks everything again. He hears Katja's footsteps. She's standing in the doorway; her hair is still tied up. She says,

'I'm doing chops. Do you want boiled potatoes or chips with them?'

Is this really important, thinks Oliver. What am I supposed to say? Do women really want to hear the answer to questions like this when they have already made a decision and we are only expected to guess what they have decided?

'Katja ...'

'Yes?' she says and smiles in a way he does not manage to understand.

'Katja, ninety-nine percent of humanity prefers chips to boiled potatoes. That's a well-known fact.'

'Really?'

'Really. So your question is pointless. You know what I'll say.'

'But boiled potatoes are healthier than chips.'

'I know that too. That is also a well-known fact. And I knew that you were going to say just that.'

'How did you know?'

'Because I know how much you like asking rhetorical questions.'

Katja is no longer smiling. She wipes her hands on her apron and looks at him, with a slight pout.

'What's wrong with you today? I just asked you what you want for lunch. And you seem to want to fight ...'

'No, Katja, it's you who wants to fight. Otherwise you wouldn't ask me questions like that. Either you would fix something that you want and we would all eat it and no one would complain, or you would ask me what I really wanted and then you'd go and fix that. But as it is, what in fact do you do? You come, you ask me what I want for lunch, and I tell you, and you explain why that's not OK. Does that strike you as normal?'

He could see her eyebrows trembling. That always happened before she started crying.

But at that moment the boy came in again. He was carrying his ball. He looked at them, said nothing for a moment, like a wild animal sniffing the air, and then he said,

'Are we really not going fishing today, Daddy?'

Oliver went on sitting there, looking at the two of them. Katja was looking at him sadly and reproachfully. The boy was looking at him sadly and reproachfully. He could not work out why they were all suddenly accusing him of something. He turned away, put his head between his hands and said,

'Leave me alone. Really, leave me alone. I have work to do.'

Katja and the boy went out silently. He heard Katja going back to the kitchen and the boy going out of the house, slamming the door behind him. He sat like that for a minute or two, holding his head in his hands and waiting, waiting, not knowing himself what for. He was somehow vaguely aware that this here was his life that had suddenly become as narrow as a passage between hellishly burning walls, he gripped his head increasingly tightly, he felt that a headache was coming from somewhere deep inside him, he sat staring at the letters on the keyboard in front of him, ran his eyes over those letters, slowly, very slowly writing in his thoughts one word, not believing himself what word it was that he was writing with his gaze, and just when he grasped what it was, just when he had wanted, appalled, to leap up and do something, just when he was trying to prise his suddenly overweight body off the chair, just as he was struggling, as in a dream, to move while something prevented him from doing so, just when he wanted to bring this shot to an end, to press the STOP button, to wind the film back, to turn everything back to a few moments earlier, to erase everything that had happened in the last half hour, precisely then, at just that moment there was a shriek of brakes, really close, a scream, shattering glass, and then a great silence that covered everything.

Nosedive

1

There is no right place to start this story. Everyone seems both equally wrong and equally right. There is no possibility of expressing it all in linear fashion, because sometimes time flows in a circle. It seems to me that from time to time something that has already happened happens all over again, following the same, senseless pattern that I am unable to prevent. And heaven knows whether I do actually try. Perhaps I am just deluding myself, enjoying this endless gloomy lament.

Nosedive.

That one word, which someone uttered recently, caused my breath to stop for a little longer than is natural.

Nosedive.

Do you feel the power of that word? I feel it. All too well.

It does not matter. One moment, any moment, has to be chosen and things said, in the simplest possible way. Like this for instance. I once read a mediocre weepie in which it said something along these lines: 'If you are a volcano, then I must be Pompeii.' Maybe that is kitsch. But maybe it is a great thought. Something prevents me from making a rational judgment about it. Because, if I just concentrate on that sentence for a moment, I can easily feel the ash hurtling down over me, my walls, forges, bakers, bedrooms, my storehouses and endless walkways.

So, we have those two words, for a start. Nosedive and Pompeii. I almost feel that nothing further needs to be said, and in all probability that first impression is accurate, but then again, here is that other one that wants to know in detail how, where and at what moment that nosedive occurred. And who, apart from me, could be interested? It is just one of innumerable nosedives. The world is full of them. Your street is full of them. Your apartment block is full of them. Nosedives, forced into ties, tights and uncomfortable shoes, are walking all around you. This nosedive of mine is just one of them. No better or worse. Perhaps just slightly more inclined to exhibitionism than other nosedives.

If you now think that I am a particular fan of lengthy, mysterious introductions, you are very much mistaken. Not remotely! It is a matter of pure cowardice. Because, the moment the introduction stops we will inevitably have to deal with the matter at hand. Chaotically, admittedly, helter-skelter, but we will have nevertheless to open something up. And I both do and do not want that. Just like the man who goes to the psychiatrist and says: 'Doctor, I may be ambivalent, but maybe not!' There, like that.

Figs.

Peanuts.

Enough cigarettes.

It is all here.

I just have to start, somewhere, from some innocent place that suspects nothing, and after that the matter itself will take us in the wrong direction.

My husband insisted on having his own towel. I do not know whether this fact explains anything. Sometimes I would try to substitute my own towel, by using various little subterfuges. For instance, I would say that I had washed all the towels and there was only one left. Or that we were just about to go away and there was no point in dirtying so much clean laundry. Sometimes I would even hang my towel, which I had only used once, on the hook where he usually put his. But none of that helped. Quietly, without a word of protest, without expressing his wishes or displeasure out loud, he would find a clean towel and when I followed him into the bathroom later I would always find that same, definitive sign of the separation of our bodies.

I was not able to understand this. There are countless places on our bodies where we touch one another, kiss and lick, but after all of that we went to wash it all off ourselves, he would always need to prevent one single dead cell from my skin from crossing onto his.

I do not know exactly how to say at what moment, after so many years of shared life, I began to believe that I would fall in love, irrevocably and headlong, with the first person who would want to rub himself dry with my towel. The towel that had just wiped my stomach and my arse; that had been drawn between my legs and, possibly, still had a moist hair on it. Someone for whom something like that would be quite natural.

Once, my husband was gravely ill. He lay in hospital for days, weeks, endlessly, sallow and withered, quite unlike himself, and for more than a month my towel hung on its own in the bathroom. It was a sorrowful time. One towel meant that I was alone and he was not there. I would stand and gaze at that one towel, leaning on the washing machine, I would gaze at the towel long enough to wear myself out with weeping. I thought he would never come back.

But he did. He survived.

And here it was again, that other towel.

I stand leaning on the washing machine again, my feelings more confused than ever. Of course, I am glad that he is alive. But that does not stop me feeling angry with that other towel all over again, with new force.

I no longer believe that people who come quite near to death understand some fundamental things. Not at all! They do not understand anything! They come back exactly the same as they always were. And they take their clean towel and dry themselves with it, just as though they had not dragged that tube attached to their veins through hospital corridors; as though all that had happened to someone else and not to them. Just as though it was someone else, and not him, whom I had wiped between the legs with a moist towel, there, in that hospital where we never knew which of our meetings might be our last.

I do not want to go on about towels any more, really. That would make them seem like the most important thing. And they are not. Or perhaps they are. There is no more important thing. There are a lot of small, unimportant things. And suddenly you discover that you are buried somewhere, deep under the ash. In Pompeii, at the worst possible moment.

3

Death is always so close.

I want to talk about something quite different, but, for some unknown reason, this sentence has imposed itself as the beginning of this section.

Whatever you want to talk about, that fact is somewhere there. And it changes your perspective. Death is always so close. And when you think that it's not, that's simply an illusion. That is it. Awareness of its proximity alters all your attitudes, everything that you had perhaps wanted to say about love; about the end of love, about departure, about adultery ... Everything becomes perfectly senseless when you know that fact. And you know it. There is no way of forgetting it.

You are right, I am stalling again. I have hit on death as an ideal reason for digressing. Just so as not to talk about what it does make sense to speak of, at least as long as we are alive.

For days my husband's arm lay unusually still on the hospital bed. He is a disciplined, patient man. That is where they stuck the needle through which everything passed into him and he put up with it all perfectly obediently. It made his arm change colour. First it was yellow, and then it acquired an almost orange hue. Like a pale carrot. It was strange. From his arm, it spread further over his skin. Yellow, and then immediately afterwards orange. I would sit beside him, watching that other, left-over hand taking insipid mouthfuls to his lips. Watching him slowly chewing. And then I would glance over all the apparatus he was attached to, I would find a centimetre of window somewhere and, like someone with travel sickness, I would direct my gaze into the distance. That is what people usually tell you to do: look into the distance and breathe deeply. That is what I did. I would breathe in deeply several times and suddenly we were no longer there, but in a meadow, fifteen or twenty years earlier. I am riding a bicycle, he is running beside me. That is what we do every afternoon, because I can only keep up with him if I am on a bike. He is fast. He is strong. His leg muscles are as hard as though they had been sculpted from stone. Sometimes I let him go a metre or so ahead of me, so that I can look at the outline of his body. I can make out every movement under his T-shirt. I see his shoulder-blades moving on his back. I see his shoulders rise: first one, then the other. When we get home, those hands will be on me. Those same hands that are now lightly clenched in fists, flying through the air. And this thought makes me unconsciously begin to move the pedals more quickly and overtake him. Now he is looking at my back, my bum, and thinking what I am thinking. We do not know that. We can only guess. And wait to whisper in the darkness, afterwards.

I knew it then, in that ward, looking at the yellow of his arms. Perhaps he would survive. But passion would not.

No one ever teaches you anything about that. The fragility of desire. The unfeeling, uncompromising being within us that can only desire someone who is strong, someone who has never appeared before us in all his weakness, someone who has never been truly pitiful. No one told me that, ever. And it would have been very simple. Along with advice about nutrition, with a list of remedies, they should have told me this as well: 'From now on, you are his mother, and not his lover. You will love him more, you will worry about him far more, but you will desire him far less.'

No one tells you that. They all only talk about a wholesome diet and the vital importance of going for walks.

4

Marriage has its little perfidious traps. The trap of closeness, above all. The trap of uncovering secrets. The trap of revealing all the stains and anomalies of our union. The illusion that it is precisely that - that degree of closeness - that we are least able to bear.

He, my husband, is my mirror. As I look at him, I see myself roaming through the house all weekend in an old nightdress, tousled and listless. Like a retired boxer. In a way that no one can understand, I enjoy this nosedive. I run my hand lovingly over my rough heels. Over the stubbly little hairs on my calves. I enjoy the taste of my nails. The taste of my chewed vanity. There is an inexplicable freedom in that. We need not do anything anymore! We don't have to make the bed in the morning. We don't have to buy flowers and put them in a vase. We don't have to do the dusting. We don't have to watch television together in the evening, or to have breakfast in the garden. Each of us, free in that nosedive, can open the fridge when we feel like it and cut ourselves a slice of something salty and unhealthy. Life becomes incomparably simpler when one abandons the effort of being beautiful, successful and happy.

Of course, none of this happens overnight. First you are in trouble and you think this is just a temporary setback. The day will come when everything fits back into place, when the socks will be placed in the appropriate drawers and all the shirts ironed on time. A weekend will come when you will make love again in the same way and as much as before. For a long time you believe that. And you wait a long time for things to get back to normal. This waiting brings you a certain dose of calm. It blocks your panic button. And then, at a certain moment, you just realise that this state is permanent and that you no longer even want to emerge from it. And there is no panic. You have gone beyond that. It never even happened. The trap did its work.

Suddenly you are able to bear all the things that always appalled you. You become tolerant towards every kind of music. You do not quarrel with people who jump the queue in supermarkets. You do not shout at other people's children who tread on your flowerbeds. The fight goes out of you, in every sense. You stop competing with yourself. And contending with things that are stronger than you. You feel like shouting cheerfully to the entire world: 'Please go ahead, you're faster!' And you start, literally, avoiding people. On escalators, in the lift, in the street. You have only one more wish. To be as invisible as possible, to become the most unobtrusive grey creature that creeps along the pavement, unnoticed by anyone.

5

However, there is one catch in all of this. Just when you think that you have cracked the principle by which the trap functions, it turns out that every trap has a new trap lurking behind it.

Invisible grey creatures are particularly noticeable to other invisible grey creatures.

And this is where I have got to now.

I say: 'What a shame we didn't meet thirty years ago!'

He says: 'Oh, but you wouldn't have noticed me then!'

And he is probably right.

I run my hand over the greying hairs on his chest and as I lean against his shoulder I look at photographs from his youth. The summer of seventy-seven, he is riding a donkey on the beach. Broad shoulders, thick hair. The constant erection that belongs to that age can only be guessed at. He is right; I would probably not have noticed him then. Or I would merely have registered that he was simply another of those idiots who wants to have his photograph taken on a donkey. Which is probably what he was then. Just as I was only a little girl who could not have imagined that her nosedive would begin right there, at the moment when that idiot on the donkey became her spiritual salvation.

I say: 'If you're a volcano, then I must be Pompeii.'

He looks at me, his eyes very warm in the midst of all those wrinkles and says, as though he knows what he is saying: 'One day you'll talk about even this time nostalgically. That's the saddest thing of all.'

And, you see: he was absolutely right.

Even that passed.

Freedom begins the day when you stop counting your nosedives. And letting go. Because, that fall is inevitable.

Wanderings

Just as the woman was removing the plates and salad bowl from the table, the cat appeared. In one bound, he leaped over the garden fence and made for his food bowl. He knew exactly where his dinner was waiting for him. The woman cried out delightedly,

'Hey, here's Lola!'

'I told you he'd be back,' she heard his voice from the house. 'He always comes back.'

The man came to the door and put out his hand to take the dishes his wife was carrying. He smiled,

'Tom-cats always come back for their piece of meat; presumably you know that much about us.'

She gave him back one of those smiles whose full meaning is understood only by people who share the same bed. They both stood there for a while, as in a frozen shot, looking at their big, yellow cat. The cat was finishing its meal noisily and greedily. At a certain moment, presumably when he felt full, he turned his back on his bowl and began to lick himself attentively. First he licked his paw and then passed it over every part of his lithe body. He twisted into impossible arches and managed to reach his tongue even into the furthest points of his back, stomach and tail.

'He seems to be okay,' said the wife. 'He looks whole to me, he's not missing an ear or an eye, his tail is complete, it looks as though Mr Lola has got away with it again.'

'Of course,' said her husband, going back into the house. 'You worry too much about him. I'll make us a coffee.'

The woman went back to the table, in the shade of

the big lime tree. It was a warm April day. There were tulips and narcissi everywhere; this was their time. She lit a cigarette and glanced round the garden. She looked at the shrubs that ought to be pruned, at the places where it seemed to her there should be another plant, then she looked back at Lola, who was now lying perfectly peacefully on his shabby blanket, blinking at her with his yellow eyes. She knew he would soon fall asleep and that he would then sleep for hours. That is how it always was. People never sleep so tranquilly, she thought with a hint of envy. Not even as children. Even then, all kinds of monsters come to them in their sleep. But Lola slept without a care in the world. You could just make out his breathing, the rhythmic rising and falling of his stomach. Sometimes an ear would twitch, at a fly or bug. Sometimes, without opening his eyes, he would get up, stretch his back, change his position and carry on sleeping. And that was all. He had no worries. He did not think about what had happened the previous day, he had no plans of any kind, he was not tormented by envy, he had no ambitions, he did not know anxiety. But who knows, she thought, perhaps I am wrong; perhaps he too has his feline worries? But still, this idea seemed hardly likely. Lola, asleep like this, seemed the very picture of absolute tranquillity. Sated, washed and carefree. Perfectly safe in his garden. She wondered whether he had any conception of what safety was. Or did he know only fear, the moment he felt it.

Watching the cat always soothed her in some strange way. She liked sitting beside him, sleeping beside him, watching a film beside him, eating when he ate, reading a book while he dozed with his head on her slippers, in a word – she liked it when the cat was here, in her field of vision.

But when he was not there, she was always anxious. When he roamed around, through the neighbouring gardens, over the pavements, through the little birch wood that began just at the end of their garden. Who knows where Lola got to, she thought. And each time she was afraid, imagining the most terrible scenario.

Stuck in someone's cellar, mewing pitifully for days and nights without anyone hearing him.

Torn apart by the neighbour's enormous bloodthirsty dog.

He falls into a stream, cannot get out and drowns.

He climbs a tree, chasing a bird, leaps onto the thinnest branch and then falls from a great height and is broken to bits.

He is attacked by a gang of large, big-headed alley cats who hate him because he is beautiful and clean and always well fed. Surely, she imagined, those eternally hungry tom-cats know that he is more fortunate than they are. Some sense told them that, she was certain. She just could not judge whether these qualities made Lola more attractive to the alley cats, which he sometimes chased, or, on the contrary, they preferred the rough ones, full of scars and war trophies? Who could understand cats? Who could understand women? Who could understand anyone ...?

'Here's the coffee,' said her husband, putting two cups down on the table.

He sat down opposite her and looked at her. She went on watching the cat, silently.

'You're not thinking, again ...?'

She just glanced at him and shrugged her shoulders.

'Please,' he said, endeavouring to sound calm, 'we've talked about this so many times. Please, just stop ...'

'But everyone says it would be far better for him...'

'Everyone! Who?' her husband interrupted her in mid-sentence, almost shouting. 'Who is everyone, exactly?'

'Don't start shouting straight away. The vet. And other people who have cats. They all say he wouldn't wander if he was castrated. He'd be more attached to us and would just stay sitting here, in the garden.'

'Yes, he'd sit here like an object. Like a stuffed cat's corpse.'

'Don't exaggerate ...'

'I'm exaggerating?'

He drank his coffee almost in one gulp and drummed his fingers nervously on the table. 'Listen, I'm really sick of talking about this. You're not going to castrate that cat! You're not going to, full-stop! And we won't discuss it again. Really. Really. Let's change the subject, right now.'

For a moment Lola raised his head and glanced lazily at them. Did he have any inkling of what they were talking about, wondered the woman. And, if he did, would he care?

The very next minute, the cat turned onto his back and went on sleeping. His mouth was slightly open, his two sharp canines poked out, the tip of his tongue hung out of his mouth. He looked dead, thought the woman, horrified. She wanted to go to him and change his position. She did not want to go on looking at him in this pose, which made him look like a dead cat. She had seen several dead cats in her lifetime and they had all looked just like this, slightly grimacing, as though in their last, dying moments they had smiled somehow bitterly at their own feline fate. As though, in the end, what they had left the world was just such a smile, with a glinting canine in the background.

What would happen if I told him that I am thinking about dead cats, the woman wondered. What would happen if we both told each other everything we are thinking? Or, even worse, if our thoughts could not be concealed? Maybe then people would practise techniques of thinking pure, harmless, transparent thoughts?

She looked at him, smiling, and saw that his face was still angry.

'What are you smiling about now?' asked her husband.

'I'm trying to think nothing but pure thoughts. Thoughts that anyone could hear. What do you think, it that possible?'

'I don't believe you'd want to hear my thoughts at this particular moment.'

'Why?' asked his wife, still smiling. 'Are they so horrifying?'

'I think,' he began, as though he was choosing the words he would utter with great care, 'that what you really want is to have total control over him. You don't want him to go anywhere; you don't want him to have any kind of life apart from this one here. You want him just to lie here constantly on the doorstep, and fit into the atmosphere of a perfect home. That's what I think.'

The woman wrapped her jumper round her. All at once it seemed that a chill wind had begun to blow and it was getting cold. She looked at the leaves of the lime tree. They were quite still. There is no wind, she thought, there is no wind, I am imagining it.

'No, that's not right. You know yourself it isn't. I only want him to be safe.'

'And what, according to you, would be the price of

90

that safety? A pointless life in which there's no desire, no provocation, no danger, no risk, no struggle, a life in which everything would be reduced to eating his fill and then lying down to sleep? Are you sure you know how much satisfaction you might be depriving him of just for your peace of mind?'

'Satisfaction? I don't see what satisfaction there is in constantly fighting other tom-cats and coming to us here covered in wounds, which we have to bind and tend for months. What kind of satisfaction is that?'

'How do you know?' said her husband, 'you've never been a tom-cat. You can't know.'

'And you have?'

He opened his mouth to reply, but said nothing. He just sat like that for a few seconds, his mouth open, and then stood up and went over to the steps. He sat down there and stroked Lola's head. In two bounds, the cat settled in his lap and went on sleeping. He was very comfortable, she could see that. He liked that, being on someone's lap, he did not need to fight or wander.

They were silent for a while, she slowly finished her coffee, her husband ran his hand lightly over Lola's back, all that could be heard was Lola's purring and some sparrows quarrelling somewhere in the crown of the lime tree.

'Why isn't this enough, I don't understand?' she said quietly, more as though she was asking herself.

Without stopping stroking the cat, her husband said, just as quietly:

'Because out there, beyond this fence, there is a whole life that needs to be explored. Sniffed. Bitten. Scratched. Because every tom-cat has a right to his own wounds and his own wanderings. And if you can't reconcile yourself to that, then it's better that you don't even try to love anyone. Ever.'

Now she was definitely cold. She got up and went to the kitchen. She went automatically over to the sink and started washing up the lunch dishes. She made a lot of soap suds and gazed, with interest, at the little balloons that formed on her hands and disappeared under a jet of water. It was all a bit funny, she thought. His whole battle. As though she did not know. Of course she knew. All those comings and goings. All that excessive sleepiness. He would go off somewhere again. And he would be away for hours. Of course she knew. And he ought to know that she knew.

Later, when her husband was already closing the gate behind him, she called from the doorstep:

'Don't forget to buy a bulb on your way back; the one in the bathroom's burnt out!'

His voice was already fading, but she heard him as she went back into the house:

'Okay, if the shops are still open ...'

The cat followed her silently into the house.

'What would you say to a sausage?' she asked him.

Lola did not say anything. But it seemed that he had nothing against a sausage. She cut it up carefully into little pieces, put them all in his bowl with a bit of warm water, because the cat did not like cold food straight from the fridge, she waited for a moment, poured off the water, used her finger to test whether the little pieces of sausage had warmed up and only then gave the cat the bowl. He ate greedily, as though he had not done the same thing, just an hour earlier.

'There, you see,' she said to the cat. 'I know very well what you need. And when you've finished, you and I are going to the vet. It won't hurt you at all; you'll get a nice little anaesthetic. And it'll all be over in a few minutes. All right?'

It seemed to her that Lola nodded his yellow head. That was quite enough for her.

She took down the travelling basket in which she was going to carry the cat and went to get ready.

Pockets full of stones

I was cleaning the bath and imagining writing him a letter. But I knew I would never write it. You do not write letters like that in real life. You come across them sometimes in mediocre films but no one takes them seriously.

Apart from anything else, my letter would say this: 'I'm sorry I'm like this, but I can't help it. I only pretend to be strong. I'm riddled with fears, and every night I'm overwhelmed by growing anxiety ...'

That is where the letter would end. Because, really, how can all this, I nearly said irrational, fear be explained? When I say *irrational,* that is not me talking, that is someone else speaking through me. Someone who likes labels, making diagnoses, passing judgment and being cleverer than others. There are people who live in order to be cleverer than others.

Did I say I was thinking about all this while I was scrubbing the bathroom? I finished cleaning the bath, not all that thoroughly, but it would fool someone into thinking it was clean, and turned to cleaning the washbasin. That was easier. The movements are more normal. I do not have to bend over and I do not feel like some grotesque female archetype. I can clean the washbasin in a standing position. The position is crucial. Although, what kind of dignity is it if it can be shaken by briefly bowing down to one's own bath? Maybe it is just ordinary laziness, and everything else is quasi-intellectual fabrication in order to disguise that laziness? And lassitude! Such profound lassitude! You wonder what I think about before I fall asleep. I think about that lassitude. And about what led up to it. That fatigue. Forty-eight years. That is not insurmountable. I could have gone to play tennis every afternoon, in tight shorts. I could have done, if I were someone else. But I am not. I prefer to think about Virginia Woolf, I imagine her for days, writing *Mrs Dalloway* and, you will not believe this, but a few days ago, while I was doing the washing-up, I realised that I envied Virginia Woolf. A woman long since dead. A woman long ago devoured by bugs and worms. It is morning, she gets up, a servant brings her a cup of coffee on a tray, or perhaps she liked tea in the morning? Perhaps even hot chocolate? Whatever, she would drink it and then go to the kitchen and talk over the day's menu with the cook. Or did that happen the day before? Perhaps just once for the whole week ahead? And then she would be left with one of two things to do: to go for a morning walk by the river or to go straight to her room to write. Either. I was very clearly jealous of the fact that she could devote every one of her days to what she liked doing. And her husband, who was also her publisher, would sit in the other room, maintaining the silence and creative calm of the house and waiting for Virginia to write something new so that he could hasten to publish it.

Perhaps I am idealising something in that life of hers. Perhaps I am idealising a lot of things. Comfortable armchairs in her study. Expensive Chinese teapots. Unique shawls from India, which she wrapped round herself when she went for a walk. Perhaps that is all too much in my imagination; perhaps it was not quite like that. But perhaps it was! Perhaps she killed herself despite all that. She left the teapots, shawls, her solicitous husband, she wrote him a letter saying he was the best man in the world and then she drowned herself in the river, having first filled her pockets with stones.

I finished scrubbing the bathroom, did the washing-up, and now I am rolling the vacuum cleaner through the apartment. The vacuum cleaner looks like a ladybird: big, hungry and a bit cross. The ladybird's snout gets into all the corners, under the couch, under the coffee table, between the cords coiled all over the place. We are besieged by all kinds of cable. There is now very little that we could do without them. And then just sometimes you see on TV some of those oddballs with beards who tell us that all these cables emit rays and that we are consequently all thoroughly magnetised and that consequently our spines are no longer straight and that gravity no longer affects us as it should, in a word, those cords will do for us sooner or later, and we would know none of that without that television programme, which reaches us through at least two cables, one for the power and the other for cable TV. And what are we supposed to do?

I know a man who believes all those stories and since he was obliged to make some sort of deal with his own children, who wanted at any cost to watch television, while he, for his part, was convinced that the television set emitted evil, unhealthy rays, he decided that there should always be a bowl of fresh milk in front of the set. The milk served to soak up the poisons from the television. At night, before he went to bed, he would turn off the television and throw away the poisonous milk.

I can already hear the people who are cleverer than all the others groaning. Mainly because of the wasted milk. Because of the alternative upbringing of children. Because of an uncivilised fear of television sets. As well as because of the worship of television sets. There is no way that those who are cleverer than everyone else would endorse your decisions, choices and behaviour. You will be wrong whatever you do. It is better not to try to earn their respect. That is an arid and frustrating business. They are the keepers of that secret and they do not reveal it to anyone outside their circle. The Secret of Correct Behaviour. It functions in all circumstances and at every time of life.

I am going to abandon irony now because, first of all, there is nothing ironic in the fact that I am just opening the cupboard and taking out the folding ironing board, and secondly irony is such a low means of not showing what you really feel. Almost as banal as that childish *yes I am, so what*. In that *yes I am, so what* there is at least some defiance, while there is none of that in irony. Irony is a pretty cowardly category. So, I am not going to be ironical. I will go back to my pathetic letter, in my head.

Some loves end like just like this, lamely and senselessly. When you least expect it. Or is the mistake just that lack of expectation? Bad outcomes should always be anticipated. But, how are people to live if they always anticipate a bad outcome? He said: 'This isn't the moment, we have to leave things the way they are ...' And he also said: 'I'm not doing anything, but time is simply rushing past.' In my day, that was called flannel. That kind of sweet-talk. I'll be your friend till death. I'm here for you if you need anything at all. Flannel. Know that I wish you the best of everything in your life. You're the most wonderful person I know. Flannel.

One distant year, some time ago, it was a lousy autumn just like this, or that is how it seemed to me because I was in my penultimate year at secondary school, French grammar was complicated, I was worried that I might not get any new boots, my parents had been divorced for a year already and my father had disappeared somewhere in this town, as though he had never existed. Mum was vacuuming the new apartment, just like me now, with curlers in her hair and she said: 'Go on, then, phone him if you really want to, but you know what he's like ...'

But I can't have known what he was like. I called him. I got the first flannel of my life. 'I'm just building my new life, from scratch, this really isn't the time.'

And here I am, some thirty years later, in a similar place.

As long as it lasted, I used sometimes to watch his profile in bed, after all those whisperings and entreaties and sighs; he would put his glasses back on and I would think, partly appalled, partly glad, partly hoping that I was imagining it, I would think how terribly like my father in those days he was. And I would also think that this was such a threadbare cliché that it was impossible I had fallen into it. All those books I had read in the meantime, all that *insight*, all that forced introspection, close your eyes, relax into your thoughts, all that, all that, and all for nothing, here I am lying beside a copy of my very own dad, sinking into a combination of smells, the smell of his sweat, which I like, and the smell of his aftershave lotion. So threadbare. To make that cliché even more ghastly, at that point I usually asked him whether he loved me and he usually said what men say: 'Haven't you noticed yet?' No, of course I had not. If I had, I would not have asked, because it is not that I need you to love me, I need to suffer because you don't.

At this point I generally stop, take a break. In my life. In my story. Driving my car. Brushing my wonderful black cat. In conversation with anyone.

The moment comes when you have to stop because you are aware that you are no longer borne along by your own energy, but increasingly dragged by inertia. As on a downward slope. While I was learning to drive, I was always most fearful of downward slopes. No heavy traffic frightened me as much as a downward slope. Because heavy traffic usually meant that we were all going slowly, a bit tense because other bodies or other machines were interfering with our progress, a crowd implied a kind of closeness, furious, but still close. While a downward slope meant solitude and falling. Involuntary flight. Almost an abyss. A downward slope always seemed like unexplored territory, and you never knew when it was going to degenerate into its own monster and smile in your face with some hideous witch's cackle when you tried to step on the brake. A downward slope always looks like someone who just agrees to the use of the brake, but we do not know up to what point. Once, somewhere, at a certain moment, the downward slope will reveal its true power and strength. Do not ask me how I know this. I simply do.

It is the same with talking. About love, for instance. If I say: *'because I don't need to know that you love me, what I need is to suffer because you don't love me',* then it is clear that we are on a downward slope. As long as I was beside him going uphill, I was sometimes out of breath, sometimes I would walk as though I was weightless, but for a little while now, since I have been rolling downhill, the words simply string themselves together. Ugly, contorted, spiteful, wretched words. As I somersault downhill, I forget which sentence I have begun. And then it can happen that I say something random, something I don't really think, something which we will never be able to confirm from what depositary in my brain it came from.

I arrange the ironed sheets very carefully, one on top of the other. For some reason, the edges have to line up exactly, every smallest part of that lace must be carefully ironed, every millimetre round the buttons on the pillow cases, every crease ... And each time I place a new ironed article on the pile, I push my hand somewhere in between the ironed sheets, where the warmth of the iron can still be felt. Solace. Something like thrusting your hand into hot sand, a long time ago, when you were a child. When it still made sense. And now here again, between the hot sheets. I am drawn to say it again: solace. But I have already said it. I can write it countless times: solace, solace, solace, solace ... And it will not help. Just as that warm folded sheet, under which I am holding my hand, will cool before I would like it to.

He was always fairly careless about sheets. He would chuck them onto the floor when he was making the bed. It was not of crucial importance to him which part of the cover went at the top, which at the bottom. It was important only that he was warm. He would have liked it here. Everything is hot. The ironing board is hot. The sheet I am running the iron over is hot; it is even steaming a bit. My cheeks are hot because of all this. And perhaps because I am drilling yet another hole in my own heart. I am drilling it on purpose, like with one of those old-fashioned corkscrews. In a spiral, circle by circle, I enter it.

I asked him why she was better.

He said: 'I can tell her everything. I couldn't do that with you.'

What is a person to do with such a statement?

The first thing that occurs to you is to deny it. Why, for heaven's sake, we have talked about everything under the sun! We have talked for hours, we have talked for nights on end, we have talked for thousands of kilometres while fields and avenues and villages passed us. It appeared, it really did appear, as though we could tell each other *everything*. At least everything we knew. But it seems that, with a new pair of legs, somehow a whole new *everything* opens up. Some kind of causal-effectual connection, if you will permit a little vulgar malice in the midst of the pathos.

Of course, instead of denial, you can always opt for the philosophical approach. Is it possible for anyone to tell someone everything? Do we contain everything in ourselves in order to be able to express it to someone else? Is it possible for someone who hides everything even from himself to tell another person everything? Is, finally, everything spoken or is it communicated tacitly? Had his everything remained imprisoned somewhere, in some limbo between him and me, and if that is the case, who knows what the everything is that he thinks he has told her? Perhaps it is no longer him? Perhaps that everything is not his everything. I know his everything. I have held his everything's hand. For years. I have walked on tiptoe so as not to wake his everything. I trembled when his everything embraced me. And now this, all of a sudden. Which leads us to a quite revolutionary theory about creatures from outer space. This simply is no longer him. Because the he that I knew could not survive a single day if he did not see me and touch me; if he did not tell me so many things. And now so many days are passing. Weeks. Months. And he can. Who knows how, but he can. It is roughly the same with death, you watch other people dying and you know rationally that death will come to you to one day, but, deep within you, you never believe it, never. In vain do old ladies lament, sitting in front of their houses, in vain do they say they can hardly wait to cross over to the other side. It is all a lie. It is the same with love that you thought would belong to you forever. When it happens that it is suddenly no longer there, no one is more surprised than you. Perhaps I will only be more surprised when I die, if it is still possible to be surprised on the other side.

Almost everything is now tidy. A tidy house brings calm into my head. I know that it is all an illusion, another of those tricks of the outside world, and all that is left me is to make the familiar acerbic jokes with myself about whether the house is in chaos or the chaos in the house. I am putting off the moment when I will go to take a look at myself in the mirror and, finally, wash my face and brush my hair. Because I know that I will see that unexpected face again. I still clearly remember my own face of fifteen, twenty, thirty years ago. Inside, somewhere deep within me, I still see myself like that. And every day, when I catch sight of my face in the mirror, and particularly if that happens at night, under the unnatural yellowish light that adds a little eeriness to my years, I shall be surprised all over again. I look at the yellowish face there with a mixture of interest, disgust and surprise. That being, only traces of which resemble me, and which looks a bit like my mother when she was very tired and in a very bad mood. I do not look at that face for long, I do not have the nerves for that, I admit, I just glance fleetingly at it, raise my eyebrows in surprise, laugh at myself and look away.

Instead of that, it is far nicer to think of the moment when I saw him for the first time. I can run that scene in my head endlessly often, and never get bored. A moment, which means nothing to anyone else in the world, apart from me. He gets out of his car. Actually his head emerges, then his shoulders, then the top half of his body, and then he stands up and comes towards me. I do nothing; I just stand beside my car. The lower half of my body is hidden by the door, as behind a screen, as though I had, somehow unconsciously, realised that, in that part of my body, I had suddenly become exposed. I do not dare to move, to come out from behind my screen. He comes towards me. Slowly, but he does come. There are not many steps. Eight, nine, twelve at the most and then he will be standing here, on the other side of my tin screen. Or will I have dared shut the door by then and expose myself to his gaze?

He looks at me somehow seriously and calmly. No smile. No impatience. Otherwise, people scatter smiles around quite uncritically. Someone once said that a smile was a good addition to any kind of communication and here they were, everyone smiling at everyone else, even when it meant literally nothing. He did not smile. Not in the least. Not even with his eyes. He looked very serious and very concentrated. Later, when I got to know him better, I realised that this was the expression he wore when he was disturbed, but I could not know that then. Then I thought he was calm and that in some incredibly superior way he did

103

not ever try to appeal to the people around him.

Today, from this perspective, who knows how he would see everything that happened to us, then and later. The other side of truth is not falsehood. The other side of truth is usually some other truth. And in that other truth, his, who knows how I seem as I stand hidden behind the car door, in my shabby green duffle coat. And who knows how I was looking at him. Afterwards he told me that I said a lot of things that day that nearly made him turn and walk away.

All this time I have been avoiding admitting something to you. Perhaps for someone this would be the most important thing. For some perhaps even critical. Namely, ten, at most fifteen minutes from the moment when I was standing badly protected by the door of my car, just ten or fifteen minutes later, he already had the opportunity to overhear my orgasm for the first time and whisper to me: 'Give me your breath, give me your breath ...'

And now here I am, I fold up the ironing board and I am a little breathless. My breath went off somewhere into him, in the comic conviction that this man would always be here, really close, and that whenever it was necessary I would be able to go up to him and breathe in as much as I needed.

In the first weeks after he left it seemed to me that what would be hardest to bear would be the fact that we were no longer making love. My body agonised more loudly and dramatically than my soul. It was almost angry with him, my body was. Like a dog when you take a juicy bone away from under its nose. Try doing that with a dog, and you will understand what I am saying.

Then my body slowly calmed down. It got

used to it. It stopped whining so loudly. And some other tones came in. It seemed to me that I would be able to bear everything, if I could only see him, here and there, even at a distance, even at night, when he was asleep. My eyes were used to him. They were used to resting on the uneven surface of his face. Photographs did not help much. They were very like him, but they were not him. Just a two-dimensional trace in the memory. The trace of something that had already passed. A photograph was a moment that had long since disappeared, and as too much connected with him contained that foreboding of time past, photographs could never soothe my desire to see him.

Later – I do not myself know how – that passed as well. I realised that I could live without making love to him, and that I could live without seeing him. It was pretty unreal, but I could do it. A person gets used to the most improbable things. But my thoughts, I never did succeed in stopping them going towards him. In my thoughts, I was constantly chatting with him. Every day. And I wrote him those imaginary letters. And I tried to hear his imaginary answers. In my thoughts we never stopped talking. In my thoughts I still believe that his thoughts come towards me, with the same force, every day. And they meet somewhere, in a secret place, just as we once used to meet. In my thoughts that woman does not exist, nor does her name, which I find it impossible to forget, in my thoughts it is completely unimaginable that his lips should touch her breast. Although, if it is unimaginable, why am I mentioning it? Of course they touch it. His lips. And of course they say just the same words they used to say before, as they pressed into my breast. Life, cleansed of delusions and mists,

Senka

My brother had always been a rolling stone. Since he was a young man. No one knew where he went to, when he was going to come back, who he spent the night with. For the first few years, this situation made our mother unhappy and constantly anxious. She could spend the whole night in the kitchen, listening for sounds on the stairs, getting up frequently and looking through the spy-hole in our front door whenever the lift could be heard groaning through the high-rise block in the small hours. And every time it turned out not to be him, she would go back and sit down again on the most uncomfortable chair, the wooden, straight-backed one, with rough edges, which might have been made for maternal masochism.

My father, on the other hand, regarded the whole thing with a certain degree of humorous serenity.

'Just accept it, woman,' he used to say in the morning, over his first coffee.

'How can I accept it, when I don't know where he is?'

'We know one thing,' my father replied, winking at me across the table. 'One man's loss is someone else's gain.'

As though my brother and I had fallen into this house out of two different worlds, I spent virtually my whole youth watching my mother make cakes. By my tenth year I already knew all her recipes by heart and my mother, her hands white with flour, no longer needed to reach for her thick exercise book where all the secrets of our meals were written down, she would just look at me and ask,

'How many eggs in this one?'

And I would know. I always knew the precise answer.

No one separated the yolk from the white with greater care than I did. No one could judge a hundred grams of sugar as precisely as I could. The scales were no longer needed. I knew it all, every measurement, like the back of my hand. My mother's job was to keep an eye on the cooking time, while everyone knew that my careful, patient hand would be able to spread the filling over the layers of cake with the big, flat knife. Everyone knew that the final touch was mine. And, at the very end, the delicate chocolate flakes that I would scatter over the cake with a sense of reverence.

And when, some years later, a bit further down our street, behind that sad little park with its two broken swings, I bought a dilapidated building and opened a cake shop, no one was particularly surprised.

Just as no one was particularly surprised when one day my brother did not come home. The next day, his lunch waited for him on the table all afternoon, and all evening and far into the night, and when he did not appear the following morning either, my mother took the cover off the dish, looked at the food and simply threw it into the rubbish bin. Then she sat down on that hard, uncomfortable chair, she said nothing for several days, and then we carried on living on our memories, on the monotony that was unbroken by anything at all, apart from, once in a while, twice a year maybe, a postcard from my brother. Each one from a different part of the world.

It was summer, midday, and the time of day when there was usually no one in the shop. The housewives who called in the morning, on their way back from the market, for a lemonade and a cream-cake, had already left and it was still early for afternoon walkers. That was when Senka and I dusted the window display, removed the odd dead fly, refilled the display boxes with ice-cream and washed the floor.

Senka was a quiet woman. In keeping with her name, meaning 'shadow' in our language, she did everything silently and discreetly. That is how it was this day too. It was only the soft tinkle of the glass in the display boxes that told me she was in the shop and that she was carefully arranging the chocolate truffles on plates. Meanwhile, I was in the back of the shop, in our little workshop, where all our cakes and sweets came into being, trying to fix the door of one of the ovens. For a few minutes I had been thinking that we were probably going to have to buy a new oven, but I could not be bothered to speak. That sometimes happened to me: the sentence was there, ready to tell someone something, but for some unknown reason it just would not come out. In time I got used to these unarticulated thoughts. And I found it strange that people could not take them as read. Spoken or unspoken – it was the same for me. And if I had to make even the roughest calculation of how many of my thoughts I had actually expressed, I do not think I would be able to. I only know that Senka considers me a very reticent person. I always found that strange. So much in my head, constantly. But she still thinks I am reticent.

So, the good silence of noon, without any squealing children, or the clatter of shopping trolleys, not even the clink of a little spoon dissolving sugar in a glass. None of that. Just the soft hum of the cooling machine. The sound we lived with.

And that is why what happened was so unusual. Senka let out that sound. Something like a sigh. I could not work out whether it was fear, or pleasure, or surprise. It was as though she had inhaled as much air as she possibly could, suddenly, rapidly and weighed down by some enormous force. And immediately afterwards I heard the little bell that rang whenever anyone opened the door. I wiped my hands on my apron and went out to see what had provoked that sound in my wife. And found myself face to face with my brother. There was only the window between us. On my left, I clearly heard, Senka was breathing rapidly and loudly.

Some ten years earlier, when it had become clear to even the most persistent, that my brother was not coming back, that his wanderings were taking him ever further from us into the increasingly misty distance, Senka, by then already hopelessly attached to our house, decided to marry me, instead of him. Later I sometimes asked myself whether, somewhere deep down, I had hoped for this outcome. But, if there was an answer to that question, I never let on to myself, either awake or in my dreams. Senka simply carried on coming to our house. For the first few months she would usually sit in the kitchen with my mother, discussing something quietly with her, or she would take my brother's postcard with her to the bathroom, and then she would emerge with swollen, teary eyes. After a certain time, the tears stopped, dried up, and the whispering was no longer so quiet, the secrets vanished into the world of secrets, and, instead of in the kitchen, Senka used increasingly often to sit in my room, twisting a lock of her red hair, looking at the lime tree in the garden. That is how it was, usually, and without much noise, like the majority of things that happened to me. Just sometimes, at night, while I watched Senka as she slept, a chill wind of unease would run through me. It seems it was at that point, when everyone had quite stopped expecting my brother, that I began to fear his return. Right up until today.

There he was, standing in front of us, undoubtedly real and present. Like something I had dreamed countless times. Except that in my dreams my brother was just the same as he had been ten years earlier, sometimes even younger, sometimes a boy. But this man here was someone else, thinner, slightly grey, with unusual oblique lines on his forehead.

The silence, however, lasted just an instant. Senka was the first of the three of us pull herself together: she went up to him, with open arms.

'Come,' she said after she had hugged him, and moved away to take a good look at his face again, then she hugged him again, 'come and sit down. I'll bring you some refreshing lemonade.'

There followed a little, quiet, nightmare of greeting, confused hugs and broken sentences. Senka turned over the little card with 'Closed' written on it and lowered the blinds in the window. Then we all sat down at a table.

'I looked for you at home first,' said my brother. 'But there's no one there. Some kid on the steps told me to come here.'

Senka glanced at me, quickly, and I knew we were thinking the same thing. How to say it? How to put it into words, so that it was not too painful? And did he deserve our consideration, at all? That was something I asked myself, but I hoped that Senka was thinking it too. While we said nothing, trying to formulate the right sentence, my brother seemed to make another great stride through our hesitation:

'Mum and Dad aren't there any longer?'

We shook our heads, both of us. Sometimes things are clear in themselves. Sometimes words are not necessary. He lowered his eyes and asked:

'When?'

'Mum exactly three years ago, and Dad just a few months after her. You know that he couldn't have lasted long without her cakes.'

Senka added, as though justifying herself.

'We wanted to let you know, but we didn't know where to send ...'

He interrupted her with a slight movement of his hand, as though saying, it's all right, I get it, there's no need to go on.

'What about Mum, did she worry about me then, at the end?'

He spoke these last words almost inaudibly. Almost without breathing. I knew what he was, in fact, asking us. About all those sentences which we had endeavoured to catch, fully aware that they were her last, about all those disjointed, sometimes completely disconnected thoughts. However much we had strained to make them out, we had not wanted to hear them. We stroked a lock of hair on her forehead as though trying to return those thoughts to where they had come from, not to take them into ourselves. But she repeated, countless times: 'Tell him, tell him ...' and we nodded, not asking what we were to tell him. Her eyes were dull and looked as though they could already see something on the other side. Sometimes just one eye would open. But that one eye searched all around her.

'Everything's there, packed in that box', she said one morning.

And Senka and I just said: 'All right. We know. Don't worry. Rest.'

At one of her dying moments, clasping my hand increasingly feebly, she said his name. Several times. And when, finally, a few minutes later, we realised that she had breathed her last breath, Senka shook her hair, as though she was shaking a cobweb from her head, and with an anger I had rarely had occasion to hear in her voice, she uttered just one word: 'Bastard!' I didn't have to ask her who she meant. Nor did we ever discuss it afterwards. Not until this moment.

'Mum died peacefully, in hospital. Without much pain,' said Senka finally. 'And your Dad died in his sleep. We found him in the morning, he was lying, as always, facing the window, and his face was serene.'

She looked at me. We understood each other. There was no way to tell it all. Or there was no point. We really had found my father in the morning, but not in bed. He was sitting at the kitchen table, the top half of his body was simply slumped on the table. His arms were hanging by his sides, almost touching the floor. By that time his arms were very thin. He was not remotely like the man my brother probably remembered. On the table were some photograph albums. Those old albums, with thick covers, with black and white photographs. That is what my father had been doing on the last night of his life. He had been looking at photographs. Senka and I knew we were not going to say that. There was nothing to be said about all that any longer. I wanted to shut the door of this world in which we were living as firmly and securely as possible. And not to let anything of our world out. It seemed to me as though, for some mysterious reason, this was the most important thing. Not to give away a single memory, to hide them like the most closely kept secret. As though our memories had their own energy, an energy that kept Senka and me together.

The year when Senka moved officially into our house and transferred three suitcases of clothes and a few books from her rented room, my mother silently packed away all my brother's things and took them down to the cellar. Up to then we had kept his room just as he had left it the day he went away, but now, suddenly, my mother took everything out and said, as though it was something entirely ordinary:

'Take this room, it's bigger and brighter. It'll be a good bedroom for you.'

And that is how it was.

Sometimes, when there was no one at home, I would wander through the apartment, trying to see whether there was any trace of him left. Apart from two family photographs in the living room, slowly, and, it seemed to me, unnoticed, I had removed everything. In fact, I sometimes imagined that each one of the four of us was, secretly, removing every trace of my brother. Perhaps it seemed to all of us that we would be less angry with him if we put it all away. That at some moment we would believe he had never existed.

And only when there were no longer any of his old comics, or boxes of tools, or the few lighters that had long since ceased to contain any fuel, or the torches with which he went down to the cellar to repair the fuses, or the poster from the film 'Hair', which had been stuck for years on the inside of his wardrobe door, because our mother was a great opponent of sticking posters on walls, or the key ring in the shape of a little globe – only when none of that was there, only then could I begin truly to enjoy Senka's soft, round body.

We sat like that for a little while longer, ate a few baklavas and talked, I no longer know what about. My brother talked a lot more than us. He mentioned several countries, cities, he said even that somewhere a long way away, on the shore of a lake, there was a house he kept returning to, but I did not want to remember any of that. Not a single name, not a single place in the world. It was too late for me to start connecting any geographical points with him.

'I'll see him off,' said Senka, when my brother got up and let us know he was leaving.

I simply nodded, as I always do. And nothing of what I had not expressed came out of me, not this time either. I held out my hand to my brother, we patted each other awkwardly on the shoulder, the little bell on the door rang, the two of them went out, vanished perplexingly rapidly and I was suddenly alone. Here, in the middle of the cake-shop. I realised this was a dream I had had countless times. It had just happened. I knew that Senka would not come back. I had removed his belongings to no purpose. I had avoided mentioning his name to no purpose. I had convinced myself that everything of his had been packed into a few cardboard boxes and firmly stuck down with tape to no purpose.

What did he say the name of that lake was? I should have remembered. I shall never know it now. And I know that I would not have looked for her, even if I knew where she was. We had waited for him, all these years, pretending to each other the whole time that we were not waiting.

I took the little dishes and spoons from the table, put them quietly into the dishwasher and began looking around me. This was mine, only this, this silence, these sacks of flour and sugar, the orderly rows of eggs in the fridge, the little coloured baskets, the vanilla sticks. This was mine. I breathed it all in, waiting, not waiting, calming myself, ready to run after them, with my feet heavy and chained to the ground, I inhaled my fear. It smelled of fresh strawberries, of lemon rind. I'll go home now, I thought. I'll close the shop early and go home to have a sleep. All I need now is a long, dark sleep.

And then, suddenly, the door opened, the little bell jumped, in two steps Senka was here, beside me, smiling, and watching in surprise as I made unusual patterns with flour under the big table.

'Hey, what's got into you?' she asked, placing her hands on my face.

I just shook my head. The words never came out of me, never the right ones, and never when I needed them most. You'll have to hear them some other way, I thought.

Just as my mother had once done, Senka took a fine white handkerchief out of her apron pocket and wiped my cheeks with it. And my eyes. And all those tears which had appeared there, who knows from where. Her handkerchief, just like everything in that world of ours, smelled of cakes. Finally, I raised my eyes and looked at Senka. She was beautiful. And she was mine.

'Shall we open the shop?' she asked. 'It's been a long enough break.'

'Yes, let's.'

Sky

1

I have been here before.

I have walked through all these streets. I know these houses. I even almost recognise the people I meet.

I know all this.

Only I do not know when it was.

That is my problem.

People here are so childish. They believe that we appear in gleaming, silent ships, that we land in a distant clearing and emit signals that cannot be intercepted. People believe that we take on their, human, form so as to deceive them. People believe that there is something called a form! They believe that bodies have limits, that things have limits, that one can judge precisely how far something extends. They say: I am six feet tall. And that means something to them. That measure. That distance. People believe in colours. It seems to them that their eyes are blue. Or brown. And they see far better in the light. They are unsure in the dark. People, on the whole, connect the image of what they have seen with light.

I am beginning to be a bit like them. It matters to me when something happened. That *when*. It means nothing. They do not get it. There is no linear time, the way they imagine it. But they still want me to tell them exactly when something happened. And when it will happen again. Backwards and forwards, that is how they see things.

And form. In what form was I here before? Was I a person then as well, or perhaps a molecule? Or a dog kennel? What was I, then? It is hard to explain to them. They confuse me with all their questions. They believe that if I really am what I say I am I must answer all their questions, otherwise, they will not believe me. I do not understand why they expect us to know everything.

If I were able to make objects float before their eyes, then they would believe me. Or if I could resolve with a wave of my hand what they call illness, if I could lay my hand on a cripple and he suddenly stood up straight and began to dance, they would believe me. If I walked on water. If I shone in the dark. If a three-headed creature looking like their insects emerged from me. Then they would respect me. Then they would listen to me. People want to see a miracle. And, according to them, a miracle is everything they are incapable of doing. And the other way round, whatever they can do is not a miracle, it is just ordinary.

On the other hand, I am not able to do a lot of what they do. Nothing amuses me and I do not know how to laugh. That has worried them. I do not know how to cry and to be sad. That has disappointed them. I do not understand what drives them to lay their heads on pillows and sink into sleep. I do not need rest. Because I do not expend energy. I am part of energy! I renew myself of my own accord, perpetually. I would have renewed myself far more quickly if they did not keep me here, if they did not force me to swallow all these medicines of theirs.

They make medicines of toxic materials which belong in the emptiest holes of the cosmos. They fill me with that rubbish. To absolutely no avail. They do not hear me when I tell them it has no effect on me. They are content when I lie on my back and close my eyes, when I say nothing and when I do not send messages to that part of reality that they call the sky. But the sky is everywhere, they cannot grasp that. The sky is below and above them.

They do not like hearing the voices of my people. Then they tie me down to the bed with straps. There is absolutely no need. All I want to do is occasionally pass on my observations to my people. After all, that is why I came here. Now. Or who knows when. I am beginning to forget. I am beginning to think in their categories. That is interesting as well. How much time would I have to spend with them to become the same as them? And what force is it in them that is making my being change? I do not believe it is their medicines. I am entirely immune to them; my chemical system automatically rejects everything that does not belong to me. So, that is not it. It is a matter of something more complicated. Some ability that they are not actually aware of. I am just preparing to send a comprehensive message while I still can, while I still possess my being, the way it was sent here. Because I am afraid that soon the same person will no longer speak out of me.

I just had the thought 'I am afraid'! That is what one of them would have said. None of my people would have said that. Fear does not exist. What exists is awareness of evil. There is awareness of the inevitability of coming into being and disappearing. But no fear is entailed. Because fear, the way they feel it, is quite senseless if it is inevitable. What can be avoided is avoided, the best solutions are examined and the most logical of them is chosen. Of course, there are events that cannot be avoided. Those events occur and no one tries to prevent them. It would not be rational. But people often do just that; that is what I have not managed to understand about them. Because, it is clear that they have the ability to distinguish the inevitable from what can be avoided. But nevertheless, they need to resist the inevitable. They maintain that this strengthens their character and contributes to the progress of their species, this struggle against inevitable outcomes. If they gave me a bit more time and did not put obstacles in my way, I would dedicate a large part of my report to precisely this characteristic of theirs. Because I suspect that the key to understanding their being is there somewhere.

People are irrational beings driven by motives that are still not sufficiently clear to me. They live in constant conflict between their reason and their emotions. They have not yet found a connection between knowledge and feelings. But that does not surprise me. It took my people thousands of generations to reach that connection. I could tell them. Those are very straightforward matters. It is precisely that connection that controls the whole cosmos. But, first of all, these people would not believe me, and it would be hard for them to do so. It is early days for them. Their time is still a time of searching. All living beings have to go through a time of searching. Some beings find answers. Some never do. The majority of civilisations die out long before they come anywhere near a hint of those answers.

2

'Dad...'

The man turns his head slowly on the pillow and sees that small woman beside him, the left arm of her coat somehow wet, as though she has caught the rain on just that side. He glances through the window again. It is true, it is raining. If he could just concentrate a little, he would be able to find a message and its meaning in the rhythm of those drops. Drip, dripdripdrip, pling, drip, a thought, that message, always the same, is beginning to form.

'Dad, it's me, look at me.'

The man finally speaks, as though with difficulty:

'You're wet,' he says, using the polite plural. 'You should take that coat off.'

The small woman takes off her coat and drapes it carefully over a chair. Then, with a slow movement, she runs her hands over the edges of her skirt, moves the blanket covering the man aside and then sits down on the bed beside him. She takes his hand in hers and rubs it.

'Today everything turned out differently from what I expected. We were supposed to go today to look at that house, but they put it off and here I am with you, and I know that you weren't expecting me. Isn't it great, that I could come after all?'

And then she looks at him. She is expecting a response, obviously. The man does not know what he might answer. He would like to know, but he does not. And he does not know what kind of house they were supposed to have looked at. Who was supposed to look at it. Or why. So many questions. He tries to find the right response. He does not want this small woman to be sad. He thinks he has already seen her sad before. Somewhere in his memory, he keeps her face, leaning over him. And then strange, salty drops which fall from her onto his face, over his lips. He knew their chemical composition the moment they touched him and concluded from that composition that this must be what they called sadness.

'I hope you are well,' says the man.

And looks at her. Hoping that this is a good, neutral response.

'I've brought you something, Dad. I want you to take a look.'

And then she opens her backpack and takes a rag object out of it. She places it on his hand.

'Look, Dad. Smell it. It's Pongo. Remember my Pongo?'

It is still raining. DripdripdripDRIP, he hears, three short ones and then a really large, heavy drop, but from somewhere something else comes, something at the level of his ribcage, like a large silvery fist that goes from there to his brain.

'Strange,' says the man, 'for a moment I thought I could feel a pain.'

'That's good, Dad, that's good.'

And she squeezes his other hand, the one that is not holding the rag object.

'Smell it again,' says the small woman.

And he smells it again.

Strong as an implosion. Like a shriek sucked back into him. That is how that image flies past him, out of the blue. He sees a garden crowded with trees and knows that it is early spring, because the cherries and apricots are blossoming. He can smell their scent. He sees the occasional petal fly away, on the wind. And there, low down, a little girl is sitting. Holding a small teddy bear. Something warm. Something salty. Drip drip drip. It is raining. These things are confusing me again, the man thinks. They are confusing me again. The rain will not last much longer and if they carry on like this I shall never manage to hear the message to the end. And it is a really important one.

'Please go now. I would like to be left alone.'

The woman looks at him with an expression he cannot interpret.

He gives her back the rag object and is aware that he is meant to say something more, because she is not going to leave that easily.

'Still, thank you for coming.'

The small woman gets up, looks at him for a while, then takes her object and returns it to her pack. She puts her coat on. She lowers her lips to his face. Briefly. She touches his hand. Holds it for a moment. Sighs. Then she says:

'All right, Dad, I'll come again, the day after tomorrow.'

And she goes to the other end of the room. She glances at him once more and then quietly closes the door behind her.

This is not good, thinks the man. This is not at all good. They are forcing me to resemble them. I have only got a very short time left to put that report together. A very short time. I have to start, at once.

And then he is aware of that salt moisture sliding down his face, reaching his lips. Almost the same chemical composition as that woman's moisture. But rain is not that salty. Rain has a different composition. That means I am not the sky, he thinks.

The sky emits quite different drops than I do.

He knows that it is going to come now, unstoppable. That shriek from inside him.

> I am not the sky!
>
> I am not the sky!
>
> And I used to be. I could have been forever!

And he knows that they will come in soon and tie him down.

And that they will keep him tied down like that until he reconciles himself to this fact. That he is no longer the sky.

Get thee to a nunnery

Instructions for the reader,
particularly if he is a middle-aged man!

I warn you, reader: what follows is going to be far more like a pamphlet than a story. And an angry feminist pamphlet at that. So, if you don't feel like reading something along those lines, skip to the next one. To the next woman, I mean. Maybe she'll give you an easier time.

Also, given that it's a pamphlet, I won't be paying much attention to style. Because I woke up annoyed with a tune. And here I am, before my first coffee, sitting here to write it down. I find it hard to think about style, first thing in the morning. On the whole, I concern myself with stories and style once night falls. Then I'm easy. I mean, in the dark. I'd like to see you try this, in the morning, before coffee.

And you should know they're drilling something right now in the next apartment. However much of a literary stereotype that may be, this time they really are drilling. Everything has fallen nicely into place. Scatter while you still can, this is my last warning. Don't say later that I didn't tell you, didn't drop a hint. You'll be reading things you have no wish to read about yourselves and it may happen that you won't be able to get it up any more after that. It's getting harder to get it up in any case, isn't it? And all you need now is some harpy who will put a jinx on it, as capricious and precious as it is. It would be better for you to stroke its greying balls and take it away somewhere where people write stories that will make it cheerful and lively. Of course. The last thing you need now is me to come along and traumatise it. And as God is my witness traumatising it is not remotely what I want to do. What I'd like most, dear sir, would be to chop it off. That's how things stand. So you decide.

Oh woe, 'Steamroller'!

You can fuck me if I know why I woke up this morning with that tune in my head. (That 'you can fuck me' is just a metaphor, keep your hands to yourself, you clown!). Do you remember that stupid sloppy song by *Steamroller?*

Neda no longer snubs us so haughtily
Neda now says 'yes' more easily ...

I don't know how much disgust I can express publicly, without one of the surviving authors taking me to court. Not that I care. I'll defend myself with some of those paragraphs about works of art being protected from that kind of moralising. And then, if it comes to that, your honour, you'll have to accept that this is a work of art. Although I'd probably chop yours off as well, if you happened to find yourself in the right place at the wrong time. But since it's a matter of a work of art, you can just grin and bear it.

So, let's examine the incriminating lines. What's going on here? The hero of the song 'Neda' is hanging around doing nothing one morning (we won't ask why he's not at work at this time of day, he's probably retired, or he's out of work, or he's one of those phonies who make out they're freelance artists, which translated means that don't do anything but live off their wives) and, lazing about like that he bumps into her, Neda, *his childhood love*. And, here he is, up to his ears in sentiment:

She used to catch fire and light up then
She's changed a lot over all these years.

And he hasn't changed, I suppose? He's still that same goalie, eleven taut stone, with thick hair, white teeth? I remember. Let's go on. Neda is pleased to see her old schoolmate, possibly once even an old flame, and being as naïve as women can sometimes be, she starts sounding off to him. She thinks: she's got someone to talk to. She doesn't grasp the fact that the man in front of her is a forty-five year-old impotent in the making. Not a bit of it, Neda hasn't a clue and she starts prattling.

She tells me she's slaving in some dreary firm
She's getting tired of it, she's dying of boredom.
She says she's still single and would have no problem
If I came back to her place for a drink ...

Hey, now you're talking, thinks our hero! Now I'll get my own back for all those years of wanking and the fact that I once saw you in the gym changing room taking off your shorts. I wouldn't have seen you if I hadn't wandered past on purpose, but never mind that now. I must have wanked at least eight thousand times over the continuation of that story. In which I come into the changing room and you, Neda, pretend to scream, but you know no one can hear you, and I throw you down over those smelly gym shoes, onto a bench ... He didn't know what he'd do next, the smell of the gym shoes was already making him come. And he was never going to tell Neda that. What mattered now was that she had grown older. That filled him with blissful peace. And amazing self-confidence.

One drink, another drink, a lot of compliments, a few memories and the occasional anecdote from those days, and our Neda is thoroughly primed. And how could she not be. Presumably after all these years she'd learned how to protect herself from pregnancy. And her mother wouldn't phone to see why she wasn't home yet. So the scenario is more or less predictable.

I watch her get undressed in an expert manner
and ask if she remembers those distant days
how she refused every one of us
she laughs and says I was very young...

She's making herself quite clear. That she has matured and learned a thing or two along the way. That she's stopped being afraid of her desires. That she's learned to use her body. To allow herself to desire and take what she desires. But there's no point talking to him. All our hero sees is that Neda undresses *expertly*! Expertly, presumably like a whore, let's not beat around the bush, boy, we know what you had in mind. Because, what could Neda become, if not a whore? 'Get thee to a nunnery!' our fifteen year-old Hamlet, masturbator from the gym changing room, screams to himself, while making out that he's calmly knocking back his fourth whisky on the rocks and watching Neda undress like a pro. And she's a pro presumably because she knows how to untie her shoe laces and undo her bra, without her hand shaking. Because, in his imagination, whenever he had tried to take off Neda's shorts or put his hand under her sweaty T-shirt, his hand would shake so hard that didn't know where he was aiming and that shaking meant that he came long before he even reached the laces of her gym shoes. And how could it be that anyone, even Neda herself, could undress her so calmly, collectedly and infallibly? Where was the higher cosmic justice in that?

All right, we see. Our hero has finally laid the middle-aged Neda. Hooray. Bully for him. Mind you, we haven't asked Neda how it was for her. Who knows what she would have said. About the stench of alcohol. His rotten teeth. His hairy back. About the fact that halfway through the job, he seemed to flag a bit, and she had encouraged him as only she knew how, to get the thing done. That's not the main point. Let Neda write her own song, if she wants and we can analyse that on some other occasion. Here our hero is exulting. Here he is looking at himself in Neda's bathroom. He's rinsed his little tool, now calm once more, in Neda's washbasin, put on his trousers and shirt, singing to himself:

Neda no longer snubs us so haughtily
Neda now says 'yes' more easily ...

He's bursting with triumph, the little dear. But then again, he feels bad. He would have liked not to have met her. He would have liked to believe that Neda had remained forever pure. He would have liked to have gone to her room and given her a good slapping. Under this mournful yellow light he now seems to himself more like a mummy than a man. He leans forward and looks at the double bags under his eyes. And he knows that for the next three days his back will ache from the crazy acrobatics of the previous night. As for his stomach, it was already beginning to burn. Why tell Neda about his ulcer and high blood pressure? He had drunk as much whisky as he needed, even if it was his last. And the way he felt now, it seemed as though it would indeed be his last.

And what do serious writers say about this? The case of Klara

Steamroller is not my only source of cultural-artistic meditation, if that's what you meant to say. I sometimes reach for serious writers too. In one such serious book, our hero arrives in the town of his youth, *because a small town exists in order to be left.* All of them, those heroes, are born for far more than what they have been given, that is an axiom, in case you didn't know. And so he roams here and there for a few pages, he has toothache, he meets a school-mate who is a dentist, he sits him down on his dentist's chair, word by word, and now here is our hero that same evening *on the veranda of one of those villas from the days of Italian rule, with a stone balustrade and an enormous courtyard with palms ...* Food, drink, heavenly wines, it's all here. And soon Neda will be too. Any minute. Except that in this case she's not called Neda, but Klara. But that's it. *Her name was Klara. Even in the first year of secondary school she was among the prettiest girls in town.* You can guess the rest. Once a beauty, always a beauty. At least in our imagination. Our hero is impatiently expecting Klara to appear, he's lost count of how many glasses of wine with water he's downed and the sea air is often deceptive, and the dentist's anaesthetic is easing off and he needs something to cure the unpleasant sensation in his jaw. *And then on a path in the courtyard Klara appeared. She was still beautiful. A body, which has been a source of pleasure, a soul which has not been racked by solitude or need, remains beautiful as it grows old.*

You get the idea? Namely, our Klara too has become a whore. Her body has been a source of pleasure. As an acquaintance of mine, who knows the material well, once said of his first unfaithful lover, whoring keeps whores from growing old. That seems to have been the case with Klara as well. Bless her. So, her soul was not racked, it was only Klara herself who was pinioned on beds. More like aerobics. While her first victims were out there in the wide world, suffering, curing their youthful frustrations and complexes.

And here's Klara, she's already giggling, here on the terrace. *She lived alone. She worked in the local theatre as store manager ...* I can't help wondering why these beauties are always alone. There, both Neda and Klara, girls like that and still alone? Is that, in fact, some kind of justice? Whatever, Klara laughs and drinks, not lagging behind our hero.

She grew weak with laughter as I told her that one evening I had set off three times towards her table to ask her to dance. And that each time I had turned back at the last minute. Why, why did you turn back, she asked me coyly. That woman was now all mine. I sensed, Rudi, that something terrible was happening. As though I had entered a shrine of which only the ruins were left, the magnificent remains of former glory.

And the more inclination she showed towards me, an inclination that was becoming an open invitation at last to touch her, the more I felt an inexplicable fury. I saw my whole life in all its dreariness.

If you think that his fury and this dreariness are going to stop our hero screwing Klara, you are sorely mistaken. Because in the very next paragraph he says that he knew he would, that very night, *become a member of the little circle who had possessed Klara.* And here's a little circle again. Somewhere, Klara's lovers are counted up, whether she wants it or not. But even one is too many in such a situation, if that one is not our hero. However many there were, Klara is a whore, that's clear. And now an old whore at that. A bit tipsy.

Not to drag the story out. They went for a bit of a walk, they spent a bit of time evoking memories of familiar spots, and then, of course, they went to her flat and Neda, sorry, Klara, skilfully freed herself from her clothes, they all do that skilfully, so that our hero had an opportunity to fill her body, *still trim and lovely,* with his adolescent furies right up until morning.

And then, the morning. Mirror. Bags under the eyes. Ulcer. Maybe even haemorrhoids. Just like the previous extract.

What happened to Klara? She was left in a blind alley, in a space with a double floor. On one of those side paths that hide from us the places where our real life ought to be played out.

Whose fault is that, Klara? You saw tonight what you had missed; this could have been your life had you not been so haughty. If you had not yourself chosen to remain on that side path. Fury is eternal and nothing will soothe it. No high quality Italian wine.

No kisses. No spilling of semen into the desire of one's youth. There is no anaesthetic for this situation.

In the interests of serious research we will consider another literary case. Tamara.

In a nice story, if it is indeed a story and not a dream, there is a certain Tamara. Who is not, in fact, called that, but the hero permits us to call her that, because, in his opinion, the name suits her. So we will call her Tamara. *I could call her whatever I like, she would immediately know I meant her,* says our hero. And he says too that this name suits her well because it is somehow *enduringly young.* Whatever that means.

Our hero had known Tamara, if she was indeed Tamara, since his earliest childhood. And her childhood was complicated and over-full of details, which you don't want to hear about here. Her father's mistress, her parents' traumatic divorce, then somewhat later Tamara's first lovers, including our hero. That's the first significant difference between Tamara and her colleagues Neda and Klara. Namely, Tamara gave herself to our hero. She didn't exactly devote all her youth to him, but the mass of men to whom she gave herself included him. At least he did not need to masturbate imagining what it would have been like. Which still doesn't lessen her guilt. Because she didn't realise that he was the only one of all those kids to see and understand her true beauty.

And so life went on. Tamara would give him a jolt from time to time, she would appear out of the blue, after several years, his heart would bleed all over again, and then she would vanish again. People said that she was in some foreign country, married to now this, now that wealthy man. Our hero doesn't tell us that so explicitly, but if we're wise readers, and we are, then it won't be difficult for us to conclude that Tamara made good financial use of her looks. He doesn't say that she was a whore either, but since we are inclined to judge easily, we will add that ourselves.

Then the following occurs. Tamara calls our hero one night, and, not explaining much, gives him instructions about where to go for a visa and a plane ticket, all in the space of one day, and says that she will wait for him in such and such a country, because she has great need of him. We guess that Tamara is a powerful woman. How else could she sort out a ticket and a visa overnight, I ask you? Tamara always knew exactly what she wanted and she always got it. From her earliest years. Here's the proof.

Is it possible for love to turn into something else? Probably not. Certainly not. We were, then, two bodies that had found each other, two human youngsters not yet trained for life. It is true that she knew what she wanted and that has remained an enduring quality, her nostrils were, then, more sensual than mine, she reacted better to smells, was appalled by the wrong ones, and always got exactly what she wanted, and whenever she wanted, me particularly, and as for me, I was a bit forlorn and nervy, and I'm like that to this day.

Objective reader, pay attention to that part *she always got exactly what she wanted, and whenever she wanted, me particularly* because that is the part that will turn out to be decisive in future developments.

It turned out that, somewhere over there

in some Hamburg or other, yet another of Tamara's wealthy husbands had just died and she had wanted our hero to offer her a bit of solace. The way only he knew how.

When I got to Hamburg, it was raining: what else could one expect in Germany.

That's presumably to let us know that he didn't care about anything. As though we're naïve. Because as soon as Tamara appears in the hotel, our hero instantly forgets all about the grey sky, while she, *standing tall and with a confident step, dressed in a faultless black suit, her hair tied back in a pony-tail, which made her look younger, set off towards the large glass doors.*

So, her pony-tail made her look younger. Younger than what? Than what someone like Tamara had any business to be? Younger than what would be a measure of good taste? Younger than herself? It's not explained, but just left open for us to guess. And then, that confident step. Ought she to step unconfidently? Is there a proper way for a childhood love to step, without it being either the uncertain tread of a half-tipsy wrecked whore or the self-assured step of a rich and beautiful Hamburg widow? What would be the happy mean? When I discover that, I will be half way to discovering the essence of the universe.

In a word, Tamara led him to her luxurious and tastefully furnished house where he stayed as her guest for several days. In the hope that he would comfort her. The way only he knew how. But, no such luck. Tamara can't always get *exactly what she wants, and when she wants it.*

I've learned how it all goes, that business with love, and pain. The first time, we are fascinated by the encounter, as though we had seen God (perhaps we had, perhaps that was God, when I saw Tamara for the first time, I don't remember, it was a long time ago), the second time we want to repeat the first time, but that never happens, it can't happen, we are already cured of disbelief. And the third time, the third time we sit and try to explain to each other what, exactly, has happened to us.

And so Tamara was left with no husband and no solace. Justice triumphed yet again. Although, *I tossed and turned for a long time, I must have fallen asleep just before dawn.* But, the important thing is that justice was satisfied. *I waved to her, she waved back and I set off towards my terminal. In the plane I sat on my own, and took advantage of this to get completely wasted, thoroughly and methodically, with full material and moral responsibility.*

It turns out, in the final analysis, that Neda and Klara's sin lay in the fact that they didn't give themselves, while Tamara's was that she did. Whichever way you look at it, you're wrong. A nunnery, after all, turns out to be the one desirable variant. If you don't want them to hate you and to write and sing about you until their ink dries up, until the strings on their guitars break, until their keyboards burst into flower from that fury born in the gym changing room. Or on a warm street where the people stroll in the evening sun. Or because of a breeze that, thirty or so years earlier, lifted a pleated skirt in the direction beyond which lies only a dead faint.

Enough prevarication - let us turn to a non-literary instance. Master of tantric sex.

He specialised in ladies of a certain age. When I say he specialised, I mean just that. Unlike the majority of his grey-haired contemporaries, in the street he simply didn't notice good-looking girls with pointy breasts and firm arses. He ignored them like a mild pain. He left them to the naïve young men who could still bear having knives thrust into their souls. But on the other hand he spotted any who were at least forty-five from a distance and scrutinised them closely.

He had studied all the manuals about love-making that he could find in second-hand shops and flea-markets. He practised everything, the dirty old man. He's still rampaging. He's not even bothered by the fact that his striking performance has declined a bit with the years. Despite that, if you come across him anywhere, if he subjects you to his treatment, you'll remember him as the best lover of your life and you'll never stop regretting him.

Scene One: He wakes my nipples from their sleep of several decades – they were never overly sensitive to touch, but it turns out that they are, if only it's the right touch. It's sad to discover this at my age.

Scene Two: His soft lips suck into him each of my toes one after another, delighting in their taste as though it were a matter of the finest sweet. After a time, I begin to feel as though I was made of chocolate.

Scene Three: He is crying in one of the dozens of motels in which we have rolled, he's a bit drunk, and he tells me that he didn't make love until he was twenty-two. Why only then, I ask. No girls wanted him. They simply didn't notice him. And he desired them to an unbearable degree. Their haunches. Their breasts. Their mouths and earlobes. He could not so much as touch any of that. And somewhere around that time, he began to hate them.

Scene Four: Each time I'm about to come, he stops for a moment and delays my orgasm. A bit longer. And a bit longer. And a bit longer. There were several occasions when I thought I was going to expire, no kidding. He tried to stop me expiring. But he did hold me there, on the edge of death, he really did.

Scene Five: The sheet under us is wet through. From everything. I'm beginning to think that nothing in the world makes sense to him apart from sex. That one should withdraw to some barren island, feed oneself on coconuts and bananas and screw to the point of annihilation. With him, of course. I can't detach myself from him now. As far as I'm concerned, he can do whatever he likes with me. He can drag me like a ball around his ankle. He can tie me to this bed and leave me to wait, as long as I know that he will return at some point. He can wipe himself on me, like a towel, for I'll revel in the smells he leaves after him. And I'll lick them for a long time, like a besotted dog. He can sweep me off to wherever he likes: now is the moment. But he won't. I know he won't. He has to move on, to get his own back.

Scene Six: Every night I sit in the car, hidden by the crown of a great oak and wait for him to appear in front of his house. Sometimes his step is weary, and sometimes he has with him a new middle-aged lady. The prize-winner. It doesn't matter whether they're good-looking or not. What matters is that they start yearning for his fingers and tongue. It's important that they have in their nostrils the capacity to recognise his scent. One night I'll leap out of the darkness and hurl myself at the two of them, with a knife. There's no question. It's just a matter of choosing the moment. For the time being he believes that I only wrote that for literary effect, or in order to reduce his already pathetic erection to the most pathetic limits. You never know. Everything is possible.

The last scene, the one we started with: I wake up with that stupid song by *Steamroller* on the brain. And suddenly it's all here. That anger with writers. With the youth that they resent. With men. With all those women who never gave it when they should have done, or who did, and that's why I'm lying here now by myself with no one to lick my toes and wake me the way I like. There's no other way. Hatred for the sake of hatred. The writers are right, love has shown us God. And now we're going to kill God and go off into the next world like sinners, which is what we've always been.

Snickers

My best story comes to me only at those moments when it's completely safe, when I can't do anything with it, when there's no danger of it being wrapped up in letters, words and paragraphs. Like that pretty girl who drifts along the promenade in her blue summer dress with flowers, and disappears before anyone is able to grab her and drag her into the darkness, so my best story comes only when I'm completely powerless, in those few moments before I fall asleep. And as soon as I make out its outline in the darkness, I embark on a dialogue with myself approximately like the one below:

'I ought to get up and write it down, that's a fact. It has come now; it won't be there in the morning any more. Make me get up, please.'

'But of course, you have to get up. Get up!'

'Okay, just give me a minute and I'll get up. But I was just feeling so nicely drowsy.'

'A real writer would get up. A real writer always has a notebook and pen beside him. You've never had that. Just a heap of remote controls. Shame on you!'

'Maybe I could just go on lying here like this, thinking it over? I'll remember everything and write it all down in the morning.'

'Of course you won't be able to remember anything. You always believe you're going to remember, you relish the fact that you'll have a complete story in the morning, but that's never going to happen. In the morning it'll just evaporate.'

'That's why I'm saying you have to get up and write now!'

'No, that's what I'm telling you. And you're saying maybe you don't have to get up. Enough playing, get up and write!'

'Okay.'

'What do you mean? Get up at once. Or you'll fall asleep.'

'Okay.'

'There's no way you're going to get up. You've never done it so far when you've been in this phase and you won't do it now. Your best story will slip away from you again.'

'Who knows why it's good.'

'It's hard for anyone to know...'

'But I can see it. I know everything about it. I know its every word.'

'I'll question you in the morning.'

'Go ahead.'

'Sleepy?'

'Mmm.'

'You've nodded off. You loser.'

'No, I haven't, I'm making a note of it all in my head.'

'You're sleepy. You've had it. And see how lovely it is. Something as lovely as this may never come to you again. This happens once in a lifetime. And you're going to sleep through it?'

'Who cares. Maybe it's not all that lovely, maybe it just seems that way to me because I'm sleepy. Some centres in my brain are cutting out, one by one, I'm sure I'm just imagining that it's lovely, while it's probably just some banal sentence, plucked out of today.'

'Carry on rationalising. You know that's not how it is. It's no ordinary sentence. It's your best story ever. And you're never going to write it. Who're you kidding?'

'You're right. Who gives a fuck. Night night.'

I wake up exhausted and with a stiff neck. That was one of those revolting nights when I felt guilty because I hadn't got up after all. The whole night, sentences. Crazy, unconnected sentences, which my ear had once caught, somewhere, and I had thought *Yes, there, that's just where the story is!* And then I wandered off somewhere because I was too busy or too lazy or stuck at a traffic light between amber and red.

Eat your heart out, big-mouth! I'm holding you in my head and doing whatever I want with you.

Sentences like that, for instance. No one knows where they come from, or where they, actually, happened. But they stay here, in my brain.

Sugar, what's your problem? We said no cellophane. You said it was best like this, that's what you want. And you're just beginning to unwrap yourself; I'm just about to lick that sweet little chocolate, when you pack yourself up again! For goodness sake, I feel like those people who look for forgotten landmines. Except that I can't put my foot down anywhere without an explosion in my head.

I remember that one particularly. Sugar, ugh, how I hated it when he called me that. For three years I managed to resist writing a story about that jerk, but the sentence remained. Like ants in the kitchen, that's how those words sometimes emerge, out of the blue.

Come on, for heaven's sake, fill in those holes in the road once and for all so that a person can get home! Find some other street to rest on your spades in!

If you look at it like this, in the light of day, those sentences aren't anything much. Even if I arrange them in alphabetical order, they still look

had any effect on R. All this is putting great pressure on R. And R is a person you can rely on. At last, R is leaving. As it's his turn. And I'll end up in gaol. At R's insistence, it's a woman. Astonishing R himself. After all the effort to dissuade him. At every step, he's trying. Anything you like, only not this. At the last minute, he discovered. As luck would have it, no one. At the same time. At first-hand, I felt that. At my own risk. Apart from all of that. After all, what makes you say that? After that, R said that this was the motive. At the end of the day, it's a waste of space. After the way they behaved. And this is borne out by the fact that. And the circumstances. All those issues need to be resolved. A lot of people would envy us that. And that was that. All that goes to show. All in a day's work. And to the general consternation of all his friends. At your disposal. And they've deserved it. And what is the basis for your optimism that. Any time. Anything you say. Anyone is welcome. Anywhere you want. Anything goes. Anything else? Any time at all. Anyone knows that. Anywhere in the world. Again and Again. Against all the odds. About time too. About all we know. About a boy. Above all. Above board. Assuming you know about that. Assuming you think the same way. Assuming it's all clear now. Assuming it's not too much to ask. Assuming you won't have any objection. Assuming it isn't too immodest of me. Assuming you won't refuse. Assuming my readers won't object to that. Assuming that's not the case. Assuming you might think I'm being personal. Assuming you do understand what I mean. Assuming that was always the case. Assuming you will permit me to explain why I decided to. Assuming you can spot certain points of contact with. Assuming we'll be able to verify that.

Are you expecting something? Are you ready for that? Are they all there? Are they coming too? Are you going to have a go? Apparently they are. Apparently they want to. Apparently he's going to. Apparently, it's now perfectly clear that. As they say. Above all. Above our heads. Abandon that thought now. Abandon any further hope. Abandon them if you must. Ability is not enough. Able-bodied youngsters only. Aboard the ship. Along the way. Alongside me. Above all, that's all R is allowed. All the worst is behind us now. Absolutely. Absolute rest is recommended. Absolutely all R needs now is. Absurd but true. Abundant evidence suggests. All R has to do is. After the experience of many people. After a whole series of incidents. After seven years of silence. After he registered for a degree. After a moment that lasted an eternity. After the formalities which were anything but. After some time had passed. Apart from that. Apart from the rest of them. Apart from the weather. Accepting that this is the case. Accepting that R seemed to have changed a lot. Abjectly. A great shame. A tense atmosphere. A game of chance. A lot to take in. At least he knows. At last I decided to. A last look. A lot of evidence was produced. Accidentally in some cases. Acceptable, though. According to the judge. Accordingly, it could happen that. According to all the proof. And yet R is still. Admittedly, he said so himself. Admittedly not to me. Admittedly it's a long shot. Admittedly, not all of them can. Acting on a hunch. Acting out of self-interest. Acting for us all. Acting a difficult part. Acting rather strangely. Acting on R's behalf. Actually that's not quite all. Actually it's hard to. Adding it all together. Adding to the confusion. Adding one thing to another. Amounting to very little. Actually that's the crux of R's problem. Advance warning. Advancing carefully. Advance at your peril. Advancing a different case altogether. Advice would be welcome. Advisedly cautious. Affecting us all. Afterwards it was clearer. Afterwards he had a chance to rest. After all we'd been through. After an age. After all, what can you expect? Against all odds. Against great opposition. Against my will. Ahead of the game. Ahead of the crowd. Ahead lies nothing but trouble. Aim for the stars. Aiming high is the best we can do. Aimlessly drifting. Alarmingly lost. Alienated. Abandoned. Altogether.

And so it went on, all night. At one moment, just before dawn, the logical question – who is R? – came to my mind. Has R really been accused of premeditated murder, and who, in fact, has he killed? Is it possible, in that case, to rely on R? What is it that R ought to have done in order for the story to make any sense? Why has R become so lethargic? All questions to which I don't yet have an answer. What does R have to do with my best story, if he does have anything to do with it? It's also possible that he's just here to get in the way of its coming into being; no possibility can be excluded. In the last analysis, R is the same person who once spoke the following sentence: 'Well, if, by some strange chance, I ever found myself on a planet on which my talent for devouring five burgers in three minutes was proclaimed an astonishing gift, and if the inhabitants of that crazy planet were to give me the title of *Champion Burgerscoffer*, and a pot of money, then my character would be in a position to choose: *I'm a genius!* Or: *These guys are demented!*'

It's abundantly clear that in creating my best story I can't rely on a character like that. Which puts me in a really awkward position. And forces me to turn to a completely different scene. Promising from the outset.

He was sitting on a stone garden bench, with petunias wilting in the sun, watching the girl fixedly, which was beginning to make her uncomfortable. She was waiting for a friend, who was late for the usual reasons – she hadn't tied her laces in time or she was drying her hair or she had just missed the bus, whatever – and at first she had not been aware of that uninterrupted gaze, but then she turned towards him as though someone had pulled her by the hair and saw him staring. After that he didn't take his eyes off her. A few years earlier, she would have played the fool and simply hidden behind a statue or a tree, but now she went up to him and asked: 'How long is it?' He thought for a bit and then answered calmly: 'Like a Snickers and a half. I mean a double bar, not one of the small ones.'

'You didn't have to bore us rigid for six pages just for everything to be reduced to a Snickers bar at the end,' says R who, in fact, is not an imaginary character. He's been here the whole time; I just give him various forms to make his life more interesting. And he falls back on the bed, laughing. 'A Snickers and a half is my line, that's not allowed.'

'But nothing's my own in any case. I've pinched everything. Anyway, let's see whether we can make it two Snickers if I really try.'

'You're on. Let's see what you can do.'

Imagining her in a wedding dress was harder than imagining Grandad Boda from the eighth floor on skates.

Who said that? And when? I'd remember if R wasn't distracting me. One and a half Snickers or two, who on earth cares apart from him.

147

Under the guise of high-brow literature

If I dream I shall wake,
if I wake I shall die.
Zvonimir Golob

2005, Lillehammer, Norway

It sometimes happens that I find myself in a library in a country whose language I do not speak and look around me, in that multitude of books, wondering where we disappear to the moment we leave the sense of a word behind us? I roam among the shelves, like a child, I look at the pictures on the covers and open the books to see whether there is a photo of the author. Is he good-looking? Usually not. Does he have glasses or a moustache? has he placed his hand under his chin? Writers like to have their photos taken with their hand under their chin. Or in a coat with a scarf round their neck. That kind of photograph is the next most popular, immediately after that leaning one. These photos are usually portraits. As though it would be insulting to expect a writer to show a reader his whole person. But again, that is funny, because if you are interested in what a writer looks like, if that has any meaning whatever, then you are interested in everything, not only the decorous frame of his glasses and his comical whiskers.

But, okay. In Norwegian I could make out just enough words not to feel utterly lost, but still not enough to be obliged to follow their meaning. And once you are liberated from meaning, whether you like it or not, you feel free in many other ways as well. Lonely and free, among unknown people.

We were waiting for Amoz Oz to appear. We knew that he was going to be late because he was the main star of this literary happening. They were waiting for everyone to go in, to take their seats, blue-eyed and slant-eyed writers, men in skirts and woman in shalwars, there were all sorts there. And they were all wearing that appropriate I'm-so-glad-to-be-here smile. That is the smile that is most often used at international gatherings and is directed even towards people you have never seen before, and are never intending to see again. But, since you belong to the same branch, this almost conspiratorial smile tells the person beside you that he is here, among his own kind. That is all total idiocy; of course, a writer is never among his own kind, ever, anywhere, but at such gatherings writers like to imitate the manners of diplomats. Heaven knows why.

I was sitting somewhere there between books about Fritjof Nansen's polar explorations and encyclopaedias about reindeer. I could glance at all those pelts at any moment, that was consoling. At least until Amos Oz arrived.

And then something happened that usually happens at such a moment in stories and films. That is the so-called suspecting nothing moment. If it is a film, the music hints that something significant is about to happen and the audience, willy-nilly, pays attention, starts expecting something. But the reader has no idea. He had just settled down among the arctic explorers' pelts, when, suddenly! Shot of the library door. A tall male figure shakes snow from his umbrella then folds it up. He looks around and then notices a long container full of umbrellas. He does not hesitate for an instant and puts his wet umbrella among the rest. Then he runs his fingers through his hair, takes off his glasses, stands thoughtfully, ah, yes, his handkerchief is in the right-hand pocket of his jacket, he takes the handkerchief out, opens it somewhat theatrically and then starts to wipe his glasses, which are a bit moist and misted. He does that carefully for a while, still just inside the door, but close enough for me to see him. When he is certain that his glasses are dry and clean, he holds his hand some distance away, checks them, then puts them back on. Runs his fingers through his hair once more. With his other hand he carries out some senseless movement with his palm over the material of his jacket, as though wanting to ensure that everything is where it should be. Somewhat thinner than I remembered him. But there is no question that it is him.

For some quite unaccountable reason, I cannot remember his name. It is on the tip of my tongue. During that time he comes in, with a measured, practised step, almost as though he was stepping onto a stage. And, the moment he enters the library hall, I see one of the organisers get up and direct him to his place in the front row. The man whose name I still cannot remember has evidently in the meantime become someone important. I hide right in the back, behind those shelves with the books about reindeer, but even if I were not hiding, he would not be able to see me, I am too far away. He shakes hands with a few people around him. From time to time I catch a side view of his smile. For God's sake, what is his name?

How can I have forgotten his name? I run my eyes over the books, looking for a name, any name that will remind me. I look everywhere around me. And back at him. He is, in fact, just the same as he always was. Tall, thin, with calm movements. It seems to me that he has been wearing a brown checked jacket like this, with leather patches on the elbows and velvet trousers of some indeterminate greenish brownish ashy colour ever since I have known him. I am still looking for some clue on the walls and shelves round me and, suddenly, yes! I catch sight of a portrait of the Norwegian king.

Harald. That is his name. Harald. I am overwhelmed by warmth and sorrow. There is Harald in the front row. After all these years.

1980, Dubrovnik, Yugoslavia

'In sand the colour of sand, in my heart the colour of a heart, I'll find you...'

Everything that summer was the same colour as the cover of Golob's collection *Doves in the Forest*. The softest, warmest blue, like that created on the horizon, where the sea and sky meet. I knew every poem in the book by heart, but still kept reading them constantly, as though bewitched. And not knowing then, as no one does at the age of twenty-one, that it was precisely here, in that sequence of my life, in that book, in those poems, that a rhythm came into being that was to accompany me always. Everything I read later in my life was just a shadow of Zvonimir Golob. Everything I myself wrote later was born in the poems of *Doves*. It was in them that I found my own face.

Something like this happens at a certain point in their youth to everyone who lives with books. The book that tells you who you are. And how you will go forward, from there, from that sense. And how it will all hurt you. *'She stood undecided as though she did not know which death to choose out of so many.'* That is what Golob whispered to me that summer, on the beach, in the shade of a big green tree.

Undecided. In the morning I would think that I preferred the freshness of morning. In the afternoon I thought that the most precious was that quiet time when everyone goes off for a siesta and when even the various bugs that hum all around close their wings and wait for the rest time to pass. Then dusk would fall and wipe out everything I thought I had known from the morning till then. Dusk resembled my soul far more closely than the morning; I felt that more instinctively than by knowing myself. At dusk, the covers of Golob's book changed colour and became grey-green. Wherever I opened it, I found myself, again and again. *'I pity you, death, who will come for me one day.'*

I saw Harald for the first time in the lobby of our hotel. Almost merged with the large maroon armchair, in one of those countless quiet shady corners, he was sitting with his legs folded under him, reading. It was just a scene I glimpsed in passing. The boy's sandals were beside the armchair and his thin legs woven under him. Because, then, he was more like a boy than a young man. And after that, suddenly, I began to meet him everywhere. His glasses peered out from behind that book in the morning, at breakfast, of all the people on the beach I could immediately recognise the golden glint of his hair, in the evening, on a bench in front of the hotel, under a lamp, where he would again be sitting and reading. While everything else seethed with movement, flickering, noise, he looked more like a photograph than a real person. Motionless, present, but entirely somewhere else.

Today, as I write this, I can no longer remember exactly when and how we began to talk. And I do not want to make it up, I have already put too much untruth into my books, and not a single invented word should be said about Harald. The book Harald was reading were the poems of Boris Pasternak. The book was in Norwegian and he would occasionally let me leaf through it. While he leafed through Golob. We tried to translate our favourite poems into English for one another. They were, I suspect, feeble translations. But there again, everything was here. In the midst of the heat of summer Harald was telling me about the steppes and snow. About the steppe *swarming as before original sin.* About the steppe *standing, its hackles up, like a vision.* And, without knowing about my drowning in the dusk, he recited in Norwegian: *'There will be no one in the house, apart from the dusk ...'* And then he would gaze towards the sea again, trying to translate, I presume, more his experience of those lines, than what had been spoken.

Harald was, namely, deeply and incurably in love with the film of *Doctor Zhivago*. And determined to read everything that Pasternak had ever written. We would walk barefoot over the warm sand, and he would talk about the icy palace where Larisa and Dr Zhivago went to spend their last days together. And it seemed to me that I could feel that cold everywhere in my bones. When he spoke about that film, Harald's fingers would themselves become icy, and however much we had soaked up the sun before that, just one touch was enough for me to feel all that. The steppe and the snow. The steppe and separation. Separation and death. Hundreds of burning, sunburnt people would be strolling around us in the evening along the main street, the Stradun, but we were not aware of them. Because Harald would be relating the moment in the film when the weary, aged Yuri Andreevich thought he saw Lara one last time, when she ran out of the tram, his voice gave way, his heart gave way, and that was that, he fell dead, alone, in the street and she disappeared forever. For some reason, at this point Harald thought of Aragon and said, in strange French, with a Scandinavian accent: '*Il n'y a pas d'amour heureux.*'

We were sitting on some steps under a bell tower and I was weeping inconsolably because of all of that. The holiday was coming to an end. I recited Golob's poem: '*You are fire in which one's fingers freeze, a cold, sharp knife in the groin of the moon.*' And Harald, as though suddenly remembering something, leaped up, the tuft of his golden hair leaping too, and ran with me towards the hotel. I did not know what he had in mind, but I ran. Our sandals rang on the polished stone.

The hotel was quiet, all those who were not in the casino had already been asleep for ages. Harald was still holding my hand. We sneaked into the large, elegant dining room. There was no one there. Just two or three wall lights were on. 'Sit down,' said Harald and placed me on a chair. And then he went over to the piano, opened the lid, removed the piece of black material that covered the keys and waited for a minute, he even made that filmic gesture of stretching his fingers, he omitted none of all those details, glanced meaningfully at me once again and started to play Lara's theme. I could have sworn, then, and now as I write this, that one could hear, from somewhere, the little bells of the carriage in which Lara was going a long way away, into the snow, forever.

2005, Lillehammer, Norway

I even managed to catch a little of what the astonishingly youthful, experienced public speaker Amos Oz was saying. He addressed his hosts with polite contempt, told a few anecdotes about his grandmother who had long ago explained the difference between Christians and Jews by the simple fact that everything was just the same, except that one lot believes that Christ will one day come back among people, and the others that he will come for the first time. And how will we know who was right, the little Amos had asked his granny. Easily, said his grandmother, when Christ appears and shakes hands with the first person he meets, we'll hear whether he says: 'Pleased to meet you' or 'Delighted to see you again.' For the time being, we should wait calmly for that day, without fighting.

The Israelis and the Palestinians and all the Protestant librarians laughed, even those who had not understood anything laughed. And somewhere in that laughter Harald's eyes found me again. Just as they had always been able to find me. '*I seek you again where everything stops...*'

1989, Cambridge, England

'*From the point of view of climate, London is a slandered city.*' I recalled this sentence of Vercors, as I scurried out of the crowd at the noisy and incomprehensible Heathrow airport, blinded by the June sun. But there was no time to enjoy the gentle sea breeze that awaited me. I fought my way through the brightly-coloured turbans, the bowler hats, innumerable suitcases, hurrying to the bus station. Everything that could have been late that day had been late. And I knew that I would be the last to reach Trinity College. And Trinity was not a place where you should be late. I leaped into the first bus for Cambridge, unaware of the little hills that passed by me for the following hour and a half. I opened my folder and read through my paper once again. I knew that I would not have time for any preparation once I arrived. Now, of course, it seemed to me that the whole paper was wrong and unimaginative, but part of me hoped that this was just one of those emotions that come over me at the last minute, when there is no time to change anything.

I sped in just as the garden party was finishing and the waiters with fixed expressions were collecting the empty gin-and-tonic glasses. Ian just gave me a very English glance and discreetly rolled his eyes. I left my suitcase beside one of the numerous little tables and shrugged my shoulders.

'Plane late?' asked Ian, instead of a greeting.

'Oh, you already know.'

'And do something about your collar and hair.'

I glanced at myself in a mirror. I really did look pretty unkempt. As I was endeavouring to restore some dignity to my appearance, stepping between the rows of chairs, towards the stage, Ian whispered,

'You know, where you'll be standing, Lord Byron stood not so long ago.'

That was really a great help.

I loathed appearances like this, from the depths of my heart. It was something that had to be done from time to time, but I was always aware that I would never get used to it. I was not going to become one of those people who enjoy standing in front of a group of people, speaking. There was something quite contrary to my nature in that. I genuinely enjoyed only two kinds of communication with the world: writing or a conversation with one single person, face to face. Everything apart from that was too much for me.

Later, when the whole business of the talk was over, when the opening of the conference on contemporary British literature was over, when we had completed all the ceremonials, presentations and meetings, I could at last enjoy a gin-and-tonic. Ian flew round the large hall from one guest to another, trying to exchange at least a word with each of them.

This was after all just a gentle English summer afternoon, I said to myself. Breathe in deeply, switch off your hearing and look around you. Besides, you're not rushing anywhere. A gardener was tidying the edges of the lawn with nail scissors. There is nothing random, I thought. Perfection requires perfect treatment. The stone bridges over the little Cam river reminded me in part of Venice, but it was almost blasphemous to compare Italy and England, what could I be thinking of? A little further off, on the grass, with a jacket slung over his shoulders, was a very well known figure. It cannot be. It cannot possibly be. But it was. At the same instant, he caught sight of me. His jacket slipped off his shoulders onto the grass. He smiled, held out his arms, bent down, picked up his jacket and in three steps he was standing in front of me. It was him, but at the same time it was not. Not a trace of that boy. His shoulders were broader. His blond hair was streaked with grey threads. His eyes were the same. The way his nostrils flared when he smiled, that was the same as well. But something fundamental was different. I cannot explain what. Something in me rushed to embrace him but then stopped half way. He held out his hand, I held out mine. Then he planted a restrained kiss on my cheek. Good. That is that, I thought, we are no longer the same kids from the beach. That has to be acknowledged in some way. Okay.

Harald simply touched my right elbow and that was a sign for us to set off to walk beside the river. Neither of us said anything. Every topic seemed banal in the face of that great, terrible thing that had come between us but which neither of us dared to mention. At a given moment I turned to him after all and said, because I had to say something, even if it was half under my breath:

'You're teaching now?'

'Yes,' he said, as though putting an end to that topic. 'British literature. At Oslo University.'

Rowers passed us, on the river. The day was one of those that you think cannot actually exist anywhere, except in films. Such unreal, gentle sun. And green, as far as the eye could see.

There was a wedding ring on Harald's right hand. As there was on mine. We did not ask anything. I walked beside Harald, my head bowed, realising with horror that I felt guilty. And somehow it seemed as though he knew that. And approved of what I was feeling. We walked more slowly than in those days. Whose rhythm were we adapting to, I wondered.

1980, Dubrovnik

All that was left of that terrible chapter of Harald's and my story were just fragments, just rolled up, inconsolable images, making no sense.

It is night, he and I are sitting on a bench under a palm tree, facing each other, our arms and legs entwined. Harald whispers that he does not want to leave the following day and that he'll stay with me in Dubrovnik for another two weeks. And he is full of plans. In the winter I'll come to him in Norway. In the spring we'll go skiing. Next summer we'll come to the sea together again. Our cheeks are warm with happiness and anticipation.

The next day, in the morning, we stand at the airport and wave to the figures boarding the plane. Four gold-haired heads, his parents and two little brothers. They turn round once more and wave to us. We cannot wait for the plane to take off and for them to go.

We float on the water for a long time, holding hands, looking at the sky without saying anything. Just as, quiet and flooded with happiness, incapable of speaking for joy, we lie on a warm rock, waiting for our bodies to dry and then to go on somewhere, no matter where.

At the same moment, suddenly, it all begins to happen, in parallel. We see a few old men, who had until then been calmly drinking wine and playing cards, gathering round a table up against a wall and telling one another to be quiet, at the same time turning up the transistor standing on the table. And at the same moment, here beside the garden where we are sitting, a large black car stops and a man and woman get out of it, who later turn out to be employees of the Norwegian Embassy. They come over to our table, ask Harald something, I cannot understand the words, but I instinctively understand their expressions and know that they are not bringing good news, everything is happening too fast and somehow at that moment while they are considering whether to sit down beside us or remaining standing, and while they are pronouncing incomprehensible words, I begin to make out the sense of what is coming from the transistor. Harald's face becomes unnaturally pale. *'A hundred and thirty-five passengers and seven crew. There are no survivors...'* I look towards the table with the transistor, then back to Harald. The blond lady in the perfectly ironed white blouse does after all decide to sit down and she takes Harald's hand. She says something in their language. They have forgotten me, no one says a word to me.

I am not exactly sure whether he looked at me before he got up and went off with them. I only know that everyone in the garden fell silent and looked in our direction. Somehow, with the help of some inexplicable, wordless symbolism, they had all understood. A boy with almost white hair gets up, staggering a little as he walks, the man and woman hold him up, one on each side, and take him to the car. They leave. And that is that.

By the time I reached the hotel, they were no

longer there. There were none of Harald's things in his room. The door was open, the bedding thrown over the bed. Just a half-empty bottle of sunscreen on the edge of the bath. Everything else had vanished, just like that, in an instant.

1989, Cambridge, England

Every sentence I think of speaking seems inappropriate. Every possible question. In the end I say,

'How long are you staying here?'

Harald seems confused.

'I don't know,' he says. 'I really don't know now. My family is currently in London, I'm supposed to meet them when this is over.'

He looks at me briefly, almost afraid, and adds,

'My wife, you know. And daughter. I have a three year-old daughter.'

And then, as though it was the most natural thing in the world, he turns his back on me and goes off across that meadow, with no explanation. Just as he had come towards me, but this time in the opposite direction. I watch his back and do not try to stop him.

In the morning, out of the window of my room, I see Harald get into a taxi and leave. I sit down on a chair next to the window and realise that my arms and legs are shaking.

2005, Lillehammer, Norway

'Hey,' he says, with a big smile on his face, making his way through the crowd. 'Is it really you?'

I nod, not knowing whether I dare smile or not.

'Let's get away from this crush,' says Harald.

And, just as in the old times, he takes my hand and leads me outside. On the way he takes his umbrella out from among the others. We stand for a while in the snow, breathing in its freshness, and then Harald says:

'You don't mind walking in the snow?'

'Of course not. There were too many people in there.'

'Do you remember,' he says as though we were continuing a conversation begun the day before, 'that I told you I had read somewhere that, of all the works of Russian literature *Doctor Zhivago* is the one that loses most of its beauty in translation?'

'Yes, I remember.'

'Well,' says Harald, his face shining, 'that's why I learned Russian since then. Well enough to read it in the original.'

'And, was it worth it?'

'More than that! If I had not read it in Russian, I would always have thought that it was just a great novel about revolution, suffering, love ...'

'And, in fact, what is it about?'

Harald stops walking and turns to me. He places both his icy hands on my cheeks and says:

'About destiny. Just that. There's this thing, destiny, and it's stronger than everything else. If I hadn't read that and understood, I would have spent my entire life hating myself, probably. For the first few years I hated you, I thought that you had in some way prevented me leaving and dying with them. I blamed you for my still being here, in the world, living. And then I moved on to hating myself. I felt like a traitor. And that would probably have gone on forever, if I hadn't read ...'

Harald's hands slipped from my cheeks onto my hands. And we stood there, in the snow, telling each other those stories about destiny, about books, about everything that had happened and that had to happen that way and not differently. All at once everything was clear and in its right place. The snow was swirling ever more thickly, as happens in final shots, and we dug in our pockets and handbags and took out photos of our children, husbands, wives, pedigree dogs and parrots, and anyone looking from outside might have thought that this was how some stories ended, in the nicest possible way.

But an experienced reader of highbrow literature knows that every paragraph is just part of a far larger story, which has not yet ended and whose end, at this moment, is not known.